Lycanthropic Summer

By Denise M. Baran-Unland

Cover art by Rebekah A. Baran

Frontispiece by Jennifer Wainwright

Cover art by Rebekah A. Baran
Frontispiece by Jennifer Wainwright

ISBN 978-1-949777-25-3

www.bryonyseries.com

*This book is lovingly dedicated to the reader,
whoever you might be.*

"The wolf thought to himself: 'Now there is a tasty bite for me. Just how are you going to catch her?'"
The Brothers Grimm

So Dad brought me a gift tonight, as if he thinks that will sweeten the shit.

And I asked him, "What the fuck is this?

He hawed a bit and played with the handle on his coffee cup. He looked out the window at the diner's parking lot, and then he looked back at me.

"Well, Caryn," he said. "You want to be a writer."

I looked down at the childish yellow book with the shiny gold lock and key. Yellow is dad's favorite color, even though he never wears it, and his blond hair is fading. Even though, like me, he hates people and sees through everyone's bullshit.

And then I told him, "Dad, are you fucking kidding me? I don't want a stupid diary. I want to write..."

"Mouse, I know what you want to write," Dad interrupted me. "But this is for the in-between times. When the thoughts aren't coming."

"I'm running out of time, Dad!"

Dad reached for the coffee pot and quietly remarked, "W.H. Auden said keeping a journal is a 'discipline for laziness and lack of observation.' "

He took a sip. Dad likes coffee black and only black. No sugar or cream to blunt its taste. "See, maybe if you look away from your story, but keep writing, the story will come to you."

This is why I love my dad. He didn't give me any fucked up "process your feelings about this summer'' answer or tell me it's for writing practice.

He's on my side.

The one person in my entire life who is.

The one person in the whole world who understands what this story means to me, and why I've been "practicing" ever since I could hold a crayon. I see everything as a story. This journal entry is a story.

So what I only see him when he comes to town? I'll take value over volume any day.

"Think of this summer as a writing retreat, Mouse. Different surroundings. Different people."

"Aunt Silly's as different as they get," I joked.

"Even different animals."

That made me shut up and think. I was so pissed off, I forgot about Dad's second office in Shelby. I still had that.

And I still had a stupid yellow notebook with a cheap lock and key. Like that would keep out anyone who really wanted to read it.

Still, it was a sincere gift. Maybe I could fill it with sincere thoughts. Damn, I needed a cigarette.

The waitress brought the bill. Dad reached for his wallet. It's old and worn, more beige than tan, but hell, I was six when I bought it for him at Santa's Secret Shoppe. (Stupid dumb spelling at the end. It was only the school basement).

"Ready, Mouse?"

"Yep."

So I'm going to pretend this notebook is my friend, a writing friend, since I've never had one of those either. Then one day, after I'm famous, people will scratch their heads, and ask, "Who was this, Maggie person?"

Just so you know, the real Maggie and I sat next to each other in the beginning of second grade. She wore banana curls and farted a lot, really stinky farts. I hated sitting next to her.

Her family moved before Christmas. The day before Halloween, Maggie had fallen from the top of the monkey bars and broke her neck, with the whole class watching. People cried and said it was sad. I guess it was, for some people. I was just glad not to sit by her anymore.

So, hello, Maggie.

Now that we're friends, I'm ripping these pages to shreds. Can't fool posterity if I leave evidence behind.

JUNE

June 1

Dear Maggie,

If we're going to be pen pals, we should get to know each other. I'll go first.

My name is Caryn Alaina Rochelle. I was born August 25, 1943 at George Stroger Medical Center in North Lyons, Michigan.

I live in a big house on a gated estate. We have our own tennis courts (Mom takes lessons every day) and our own swimming pool.

I went to boarding school, an obnoxiously posh boarding school called The School of St. Savina Petrilli for Young Ladies until sixth grade because Mom didn't want the responsibility of raising me.

Dad said it was because Mom went to that school, and she wanted me to walk in her footsteps, blah, blah; but his bullshit didn't fool me.

After two years of trying, I finally got expelled, technically, for smoking. (I know this because I opened the letter when Mom was passed out).

Mostly, I just acted like a werewolf around the other girls, especially Vivien. She wore plaid dresses, a side part, saddle shoes and bobby socks or knees socks, and always crossed her legs crossed so tightly, I don't know how she peed.

Whenever Vivien entered the room, I'd growl under my breath, pant really hard, and drool. This made her scream and cry. One day she ran away. She was gone a day and half. When they brought her back, she threatened to leave again if I didn't go.

So I got kicked out for smoking even though all the girls, including Vivien, smoked, especially in the classrooms. Then Mom hired a series of tutors, but none lasted more than a few weeks. I scared them away, too.

If the growling didn't do it, the stork bite did. But that's another story for another day.

That's how I wound up at North Lyons High, and I hate it. The teachers were stupid, the classes were boring, and everyone else was just plain insipid.

The best time of the day was between classes, when I could sneak a smoke in the bathroom. I say "sneak" not because I'm afraid of getting caught (I never get caught) but because I'd rather smoke alone.

But Dad enrolled me in high school and took me for all my books. I couldn't let him down.

That's how I stopped "growling wolf." Get it?

June 1
Dear Maggie,

My dad is a veterinarian. He has two practices. One's here in North Lyons but he isn't there most of the time. The other is in Shelby, which is where I'll be forced to spend this summer. It's not that far away, a few hours maybe.

We'll get to that later. No sense is being prematurely miserable.

Dad's pet name for me is "Mouse." But he also says I'm like a bloodhound. When I get a whiff of something interesting, I follow the trail until I find it.

Oh, yeah, and I am fascinated with werewolves!!!!

Every dog I see is a potential werewolf, even poodles. Every hairy person I meet is a potential werewolf.

I've seen the old werewolf movies on television, and I just saw the new werewolf movie, "Curse of the Werewolf," last week with Sandy. Every time I go to the library, I scour the shelves for new stories about werewolves or stories I might have missed.

I've filled a whole "Pandora's box with notebooks of short stories I've written and another "Pandora" box with my werewolf research and pictures I've sketched and colored.

What's that, Maggie? What kind of werewolf research is in that box? Well, I have werewolf lore, werewolf symbolism, werewolf legends, all kinds of stuff about werewolves.

Yes, Maggie. I will share some of it with you. Just not today. Because you see, I've never read a really great werewolf love story. And I've read every werewolf story ever written. That's why I'm running out of time.

I made a promise to myself in the third grade that I would write the world's greatest werewolf story by the time I was eighteen. Well, that's now less than two months away.

Yes, I have a whole box of werewolf stories. But none of them are love stories, and none of them are great.

Until today, only Dad knew this about me. But now you do, too.

So if you have any ideas, Maggie, speak up! Because if I don't write that story, I don't know what I'll do.

June 1

Dear Maggie,

Here is one of my short werewolf stories.

Carl Bandersnacks is twenty-eight. He is a trumpet player in a weekend dance band. The rest of a week, Carl works at a service station. He pumps gas, changes oil, and washes yellow-splattered bugs off windshields. The only time Carl feels truly alive is when he plays music on Friday and Saturday nights in the Big City.

Afterwards, Carl takes a country road home, just in case he nods off at the wheel and needs to pull onto the shoulder for a nap. It's never happened, but Carl is not a dick like most young men and thinks about the safety of the other drivers.

One night, a peculiar thing happened to Carl. It was the first night of a full moon. As he drove toward the moon, the moon grew bigger and brighter and more orange until the sky and the road disappeared, and Carl saw nothing except the moon.

Then he heard a howl. The howl resounded through the heavens and through Carl's car, as if a monstrous wolf was howling in his ear. He also heard a splintering crash. This scared the shit out of Carl. He immediately screeched to a complete stop in the middle of the road because he couldn't see the shoulder. He lay on the horn with all his might, hoping a police offer would hear, stop, and help him. Carl prayed he hadn't hurt anyone.

The next morning, Carl woke up the same as he did every day. He took a leak and then meandered to the kitchen to start his breakfast. Scratching his nuts, he left the bacon sizzling on the stove and hopped to the front door. He opened the door and picked up the morning newspaper off his porch. The headline read, "Werewolf' strikes again!"

But it was the text beneath the headline that made him shiver in the warm summer morning.

The body of dance musician Carl Bandersnacks, 28, was found torn to pieces in his 1952 Tegan Maximus on Lone Wolf Road, just outside of Thunder Town.

Bandersnacks was returning home from playing with the Monty Rogers Dance Band in the Big City when he apparently lost control of the car, which was found upside down Farmer Frank Schofield's corn field half a mile from the road.

Well, Carl thought. That explains why I'm missing an arm, a leg, and half my face. Sure hope the police catch that werewolf.

And then he hopped back to the
kitchen, picked up his fork, and
turned the bacon.

June 1

Dear Maggie,

One thing I feel should definitely be in
my werewolf story is wolfsbane.

It's cool name is aconitum napellus,
otherwise known as aconite, and it packs a
wild-ass bite. Not only does it kill
werewolves, but people in ancient times used
it to poison their enemies.

You do know Laertes rubbed this shit
all over his blade to help him kill Hamlet,
right?

It's a really pretty plant, and I love
how something so pretty is pretty deadly,
heh, heh, heh.

Wolfsbane's other nickname is
"monkshood" because the plant has teeny
white eyes staring out from bluish purple
petals that look like the hoods on the cloaks
of medieval monks. Their stalks are a sickly
yellow-green. Maybe my next story will

feature monks from outer space that look like this.

I haven't even created my werewolf yet, and the thought of killing him brings real tears to my eyes, which is fucked up, because...

I hope my readers cry their eyes out!

June 1
Dear Maggie,

Another werewolf repellent is the mountain ash. This tree is called rowan in England and Scotland, Quicken Tree in Ireland, and Dogberry Tree in Canada.

This mystical tree has berries in an intense shade of red in the fall; werewolves won't go near it. In fact, travelers in the olden days would make their walking sticks out of rowan wood so werewolves wouldn't attack them.

But rowan also brings inspiration to writers; another nickname is "tree of bards." That's why I ripped out some glossy, full color pictures from an herbal magazine at the North Lyons Library.

Some show close-ups of the berries, a deep red-orange, just like tiny ripening tomatoes.

Others show the full trees, the berries looking almost like the bush-like treetops have fall colors.

I keep them in one of my boxes of werewolf notebooks to, you know, inspire me.

So far, the rowan isn't doing its job!

June 1
Dear Maggie,

So like I said, I know a lot about werewolves. There are even a couple of medical explanations for werewolves. One is a physical sickness, and the other is a mental one.

The first is something called hypertrichosis. When someone has this, he or she (yes, chicks can have it, too), grow a shitload of hair ALL OVER their body.

The second is lycanthropy. Basically a person think he's/she's a wolf...or a werewolf. BUT...

What if that person is a REAL WEREWOLF? Bet nobody thought of that one, huh?

I definitely think my werewolf should be sexy, though. Who wants to make out with a mutt? (Get it???)

I wish real people could be as cool as werewolves, or at least as cool as animals.

Shit, Mom is screaming. More later.

June 1

Dear Maggie

Sorry for the abrupt end, but you know mothers. If she gave me a better allowance, I wouldn't have to steal cigarette money from her. But you can't tell her that. She is so dense. It's either the booze or her stupid friends.

I'd say her brainlessness is the reason Dad divorced her, except she divorced him, right after her dad died and left her his fortune.

What's that, you say? You want to know about my mother? Okay, brace yourself.

My mom's name is Shirley Marguerite Rochaminster Rochelle. Her own mom died when she was a baby, and her dad died when I was in kindergarten. She grew up rich, and my dad makes a lot of money, so her main hobby is spending it.

My mom is slender, like a movie star. She has big tits, clear skin, and legs that "go up for miles," as I heard one old fart whisper when we went downtown to buy my prom dress. And, yeah, she gets a lot of "wolf whistles." This just makes her swing her ass more when she walks.

She hates shopping with me. I hate shopping with her. So we do agree on something.

My mom likes to shop with her friends or have them at the house for stupid card games. They eat watercress sandwiches, smoke, and drink lots of pink martinis.

Once a week she goes to the beauty shop for a wash and set and then comes home as ugly as ever. She takes a pill and a nap every day after lunch. The rest of the time, she watches color television, flips through glamour magazines, and jabbers on her telephone.

I have a telephone, too. It's a slim pink phone, sleek and unmarred. It sits on the table near my bed. I hate pink, so I never use it. But I do have a private number and people who call it. I always answer it, just in case it's Dad.

June 2
Dear Maggie

I love my dad. He's the only person in the whole world I love.

He's like me in a lot of ways, but he's also not like me.

Like me, my Dad hates people, but he will never admit it. He's a quiet man, and he loves taking care of animals. Friendly animals, mean animals, wild animals: they all like my dad.

My dad's full name is Frederick Allan Rochelle, or Dr. Fred Rochelle, the way most people know him. He looks so ordinary, you would never believe he is an amazing, amazing veterinarian.

He always wears creased pants, starched shirts, and loafers. In the clinic, he sometimes wears glasses: twisty, bendable, dime store glasses he keeps in his lab coat pocket.

He can almost never visit his North Lyons clinic without me bringing him an injured animal of some kind: abandoned dogs and cats, occasionally raccoons.

Mostly, I bring mice. Our housekeeper Mrs. Stickney is terrified of field mice and routinely sets traps. I free them and bring them to Dad.

Our conversation goes like this: "Dad can you help?"

And then he takes the injured bundle from my trembling hands and places it on the exam table.

If Dad can't help, which is almost never, he soothes the creature's anxiety with herbs and holds one paw in a gentle hand while he humanely sends it to eternal rest.

I love my dad.

He always treats me to at least one dinner when he's in town. We don't eat at Flemings Steak and Crab or Monsieur Pierre. These are Mom's favorite places, where we order things like escargot and Jambon persillé.

But my dad didn't grow up rich. And even after he made lots of money, he never acquired rich ways or rich tastes.

My dad likes to eat at his favorite place, the Steak Shack. It's shaped like a box car and covered in stucco. The tables are metal, and the menus are covered in plastic and fingerprints and old brown smears.

We don't need to look at the menus, but we do anyway. We always order the same meal: chicken-fried steak with whipped potatoes and whole ears of grilled corn dripping with butter.

Dad's not big on affection. He doesn't hug, and he doesn't kiss.

But each time he leaves, he touches the back of his hand to mine and says, "Be good, Mouse."

And I say, "I will, Dad."

I do try. But my mom is a real cunt. She screams a lot and takes away my radio when I scream back. She waves her cigarette while yelling at me about smoking. She hates that I steal from her even though she has so much money, she'll never spend it all.

Stupid bitch.

Dad hates my cigarette smoking, too, but he doesn't lecture about my smoking, And each year around my birthday, he asks, "Write that werewolf story yet?"

And I always laugh and say, "I have lots of time left."

I've laughed less the last few years. I'm going to be eighteen on August twenty-fifth, the night of the full moon according to the almanac in the library. Yes, I follow moon cycles. I'm obsessed with werewolves, remember?

Besides, Dad follows lunar cycles, too.

Because he's that kind of veterinarian.

June 3

Dear Maggie,

Here's another one of my short werewolf stories.

Roger McLoughty is at the zoo with his snotty little five-year-old daughter Ada. She's hated every attraction, every show, every animal, every souvenir, all the food, etc.

Ada shows her poor father how upset she is by screaming, kicking, scratching, biting, and pissing on his shoes.

It's starting to get dark, so he tells her it's time to go home. Well, now she's changed her mind. She doesn't want to go home. She wants to see the monkeys.

So Roger, feeling desperate, grabs her hand, and starts running with her to the gate, which is about to close.

At the gate is a crooked old man with a crooked smile selling plush dogs for two dollars each.

Of course, Ada wants one. Roger says, "No." He's just about out of money, and the gates are about to close.

But Ada throws herself down on ground, crying about how her mean Daddy hates her and won't even buy her one measly little plush dog.

So Roger whips out his old, worn billfold, and hands the crooked man two limp dollars. The man hands Roger the plush dog, smiling a creepy, crooked smile. Roger holds the plush dog out to Ada.

Ada smiles, jumps up, and runs out into the parking lot with Roger right behind her. The gate swings shut behind them.

About halfway to their car, Ada stops running. So Roger stops running.

"Come on, Ada," Roger said, tugging her hand. "We have to go home now."

Ada turns around and yells, "Get him!"

She throws the plush dog at Roger. The plush dog turns into a werewolf and tackles Roger to the ground.

Clapping her hands, Ada runs back to the gate. The crooked old man opens the door for her.

"Where are you heading tonight?" he asked.

"Monkeys!" Ada squealed.

Then she skipped away.

Tomorrow she'd have to hypnotize another man into thinking he was her father, taking her for a zoo outing.

But that was for tomorrow.

June 3

Dear Maggie

You know how some people are star gazers?

I'm a moon gazer.

I like to sit at my bedroom window at night and watch the moon. It's the best time for thinking about werewolves.

I think about how it feels when people turn into werewolves. Does it hurt to grow so big and fast you tear your clothes and practically burst through your skin?

Does all that extra hair itch?

I think about necking with a werewolf. Would the fangs drip spit or get in the way? Would his breath smell of old blood?

But then I think about riding on his back across the fields atop a great hill and clutching his mane under a high golden moon.

He would kill, mercilessly he would kill. And if he ran out of people to kill, I'd have a list.

We would both drip blood.

And he would never harm me.

June 4

Dear Maggie,

It's so tense around here, ya know, with my upcoming prison sentence.

What's that you say, Maggie? I never explained how a stork bit me?

Well, a stork didn't bite me, not really. Mom calls it a stork bite. Dr. Shem calls it a port wine stain. It's a pinkish birthmark under my hair on the back of my neck that looks like an animal bite.

Cool, right?

Well, when my growling and salivating wouldn't scare a tutor, I'd show her the stork bite and say, "A werewolf bit me. If you leave now, I'll forget I ever saw you."

Then I'd bare my teeth and growl. That usually did it.

June 4
Dear Maggie,

You've heard about Peter and the Wolf right?

Today I'm going to tell you about two Peter the Werewolfs — or is that werewolves?

Both were named Peter. Both were from Germany. You decide if the "tails" are true.

Peter the Werewolf was a real boy who lived back in 1725. Some people found him running around on all fours and brought him to King George I in England.

King George liked him, even though he couldn't talk, and named him Peter. He'd bring people out when he held court, and Peter would try to pick everyone's pockets and smooch the chicks.

Another famous werewolf is Peter Stumpf, the Werewolf of Bedburg. He was arrested in 1589 for brutally murdering over a dozen people. Peter said he could turn into a werewolf because the devil had given him a magical belt when he was twelve.

Of course, Peter confessed this all under torture, and no one ever found the belt. So using a belt in a werewolf story might be a problem. Like, does the werewolf have to put the belt on to turn into a werewolf? Does he have to keep it on? What if people recognize the belt? What if someone captures him and takes it off? What is he loses it? Does that mean he's not a werewolf anymore? What if someone steals it? Can that person turn into a werewolf?

See? Too many questions? I don't want my werewolf to be so, well, belt-dependent. I want him to be a powerful, raging beast! And his name sure as fuck won't be Peter. It seems like half the werewolf stories out there have werewolves named Peter, even when they're not from Germany.

But these two German Peters aren't the only famous werewolves. Let me tell you about the French werewolves.

Back in 1521, some guy named Michel Verdun turned into a werewolf and attacked a traveler. But this badass traveler beat the shit out of him and followed his tracks. He caught him red-paw-handed in Michel's cottage, where his wife was patting magical healing herbs into his wounded paw.

Michel bragged about how the devil helped him turn into a werewolf so he could kill and eat anyone he wanted. And then he ratted on his werewolf buddies Pierre Bourgot and Philibert Montot.

In case you didn't know, "Pierre" is the French name for Peter. Yep. Back to Peter. But I do like the part about the wounded paw and healing herbs.

Maggie, can ya picture it? The poor wounded werewolf limps home to his true love. He lies at her feet and rests his head on her lap with his paw held out in complete trust of her love for him and her healing magic.

Wouldn't that be a great scene in a werewolf love story??? What's that you say, Maggie? Yep, I think so, too.

OK, back to the other famous werewolves.

Gilles Garnier, The Werewolf of Dole, was a French werewolf who mutilated and dissected kids in 1573. Now before you get all huffy about it, think of it from the werewolf's point of view.

The brats might have deserved it. Or kids might simply be tastier. Think of spring lamb as opposed to mutton. Or veal compared to beef. You get the idea.

BUT, is this detail really relevant to a werewolf love story? I'm afraid if my werewolf went around brutally killing kids, my novel might get banned. Now that's not totally bad. I mean, look what it did for "The Wizard of Oz!"

But I have to be realistic. A good werewolf story needs violence, but maybe not the (obvious and graphic) senseless killing of babies.

And a good werewolf love story should have plenty of raw animalistic sex...but mine probably won't.

Yeah, Maggie, I think it would sell a gadzillion copies, too. But I think publishers would be afraid to print it. Most of them are men without any balls. And even if they did have balls, their balls would be completely hairless.

Now another sicko Frenchman, Jacques Roulet, The Werewolf of Angers, also mutilated kids, this time in 1598. He rubbed a magic ointment all over his body that turned him into a werewolf and then — dinner time!

The cool thing about this story is that "Frere Jacques" freely gave up the information, no torture necessary.

I think the magic ointment part is a lot better than the belt, dontcha think so,

Maggie? So many sensual possibilities. What does it look like? What does it smell like? What does it feel like as the werewolf glides it all over his or her body?

That's a lot more fun than simply strapping on some old belt.

One last "real" werewolf: In 1685, the mayor of Ansbach returned from the dead in the shape of a werewolf to eat the town's livestock and people.

Now that's a great idea for, maybe, a second book, Revenge of the Werewolf or something like that. Like the townspeople have a lynching and kill someone they think is a werewolf.

But they're wrong. The person they kill is not a werewolf. But the "werewolf's" MATE is a werewolf. And this werewolf is fucking pissed!!!

If only ideas for my werewolf love story came this fast!

These real werewolf stories are fun stories, I know. But don't you see, Maggie?

My werewolf is destined to be the most famous werewolf of them all!!!!

June 5
Dear Maggie,

I can hear you asking, "Don't you think about anything other than werewolves?"

Well, of course. But not as much.

Second in line to werewolves, though, is the St. Martin family.

What's that you say, Maggie? You've never heard of the St. Martins?

The St. Martins are rich. Like super rich. Like with more money than anyone will ever have, except me, when I became famous for my werewolf story.

Who cares, I can almost hear you say.

Well, I do. Because it's a super-fun story.

The St. Martins, otherwise known as Randolph Monroe McCallister St. Martin the Second and his wife Delores St. Martin, had used to live in Cameron Hills, which is near where Mom grew up.

Their son, Randolph Monroe McCallister St. Martin the Third, was born on the same day, at the same time, and at the same hospital as me.

I see you rolling your eyes at me, Maggie. Believe me, I ain't starstruck, and I ain't making it up.

Mom never told me this story. Dad never told me this story. I know this story because this story became famous.

Shortly after the birth of their kid, the entire family disappeared.

As in POOF!

I only know about it because every year around the time of my birthday, the newspapers print big "Whatever happened to the St. Martin" stories. Which Mom reads and saves.

How do I know this? Well, it's not because she showed me.

I found them in a box at the back of her closet when scrounging for change, shhh.

She's been saving clippings on the St. Martins for years. Maybe they once knew each other. I mean, they're rich, and she's rich, and they shared a hospital room when I was born.

How do I know that? Because Mom has snapshots of her and Delores, sitting in their beds and holdings their babies (i.e. me and the missing kid).

Don't you find that strange? I do. Why wouldn't rich people get their own rooms?

Monroe, all the papers call him Monroe, is the stodgy part of the story. He looks blah in all the photos. He always wears a three-piece suit, a bowler hat, and a watch and chain. He has a receding hairline and clipped mustache. The most interesting part of him is that he vanished.

I told you: boring shit.

The parts about Delores are more fun. She's ballsy weird. In France, where you can get away with that stuff, people used to see her sleeping face-up, and naked, on her balcony.

But only if the moon was full. And only if it was a Wednesday or a Friday.

The St. Martins spent a lot of time in France because Delores grew up in France. Her last name was Gevaudan, yes, as in the beer — and in the beast. She was rich, naturally, and had a wild reputation (probably due to all that beer).

Delores was also obsessed with wolf tracks. After a soaking rain, she'd drink the water from them and then bathe her face in the mud.

This is completely true, cross my heart. Remember, my mom has the newspaper clippings to prove it. Complete with photos by snoopy reporters. There's one with her face turned to the camera. She's covered in mud. And smiling.

I know what's you're thinking, Maggie. She's a werewolf. Or crazy.

But the society pages always praised her elegance, style, and lavish cocktail parties, so she ain't crazy.

She also doesn't have fangs, and she not covered in fur. In fact, in that photo, she's wearing a lacquered bouffant, cascading earrings, and an evening dress.

And a face plastered with mud, even on the fringe of her fake eyelashes and on her teeth. Smiling graciously at a reporter as if she'd offered him canapés.

How did someone as dull as Monroe end up with her? It's actually a pretty funny story.

As the rags tell it, Monroe drank too much beer at a Gevaudan party, and started acting weird. At some point, Mr. Gevaudan noticed they'd both left. He found them under one of the archways on the estate, humping like wild wolves.

She's fucking awesome.

And gone. Like I said, POOF!

And probably still alive, somewhere.

Because not only is someone drawing money out of their accounts, as the stories go, someone is putting money into them, too.

That someone, supposedly, is Monroe himself.

Except no one has ever seen him, or Delores, since August 25, 1943.

That was the day we were born, me and Randolph Monroe McCallister St. Martin the Third.

June 6
Dear Maggie,

Probably the best, completely true werewolf story in the whole world is the Beast of Gévaudan. Somehow, I want to work this real werewolf into my story. You know, the great werewolf love story that isn't written yet.

Anyway this crazy animal roamed around the French countryside, terrorizing man, woman, child, and animal — before it gobbled them up, of course, sometimes biting their heads right off!

The Beast of Gévaudan didn't even look like a real werewolf. Hell, it didn't even look like a real wolf. Its coat was reddish gray. It had a tail like a panther and a black stripe down its back. It had a short head and legs and even talons.

None of the bullets worked on this werewolf until a local dude, Jean Castel, shot it dead with a silver bullet and then sliced its belly open. It was full of human remains.

Good stuff, huh?

June 6
Dear Maggie,

Wanna hear about my pretend friends?

No, I'm not crazy. They're all real people that THINK they're real friends because I let them think that. It makes life easier. Mom threatened to send me to a head-shrinker if I didn't' make some, so here ya go.

They think I'm super cool because I talk to them when no one else does. And I give 'em smokes. Here's the line-up:

Sandy: She has buck teeth, and until last year, wore her brown hair in two looped braids. She's always smiling, which makes her teeth stick out more. Yeah, she's pretty ugly.

Babs: She's tall and skinny and plain like straw and has golden hair like a scarecrow. She's also fake, just like a scarecrow. Real birds aren't fooled by scarecrows, and neither am I. Dumb bitch.

Patti Cakes: She has reddish brown hair and green eyes that she squints all time because she needs glasses and won't get them. She thinks glasses will make her look ugly. But she's already ugly, so who cares? She's giggly and boy crazy, except when she's crying because the boys aren't crazy about her. It's easy to see why!

Carol: She has dark hair and jiggles of fat, which she tries to hide under bulky sweaters. She curls her hair up with a flip and holds it in place with lots of hairspray and wide headbands. She also needs deodorant. A lot of it.

Linda: She has blonde hair, a perfect little figure, and acts like she's a shy bookworm by smiling, carrying thick novels, and keeping her head down. But she's really a horny little bitch. I've seen the way a car rocks when she's in the back seat. So...yeah.

Hopefully, they all go off to college, and I never see their bitch-ass faces again.

Except when they stand in line for hours to get my autograph after my werewolf book makes zillions of dollars.

I'll be so sweet, so kind...and then ask for their names!

Ha!

June 7

Dear Maggie

"It was the best of times, it was the worst of times, it was the age of wisdom, it was the age of foolishness, it was the epoch of belief, it was the epoch of incredulity."

I think Charles Dickens was really writing about prom night, which was held AFTER graduation because some cunt on the PTA thought it was a good idea.

The best of times? Let me count the ways:

Wearing a long dress the color of quicksilver and platinum jewelry with real garnets: around my neck and both wrists and in my hair.

Telling Dick Darrow to go fuck himself when he tried to pin a stupid white corsage on my dress.

Strolling the dark grounds of the country club at night, with only the silvery moon and the glowing embers of our cigarettes lighting our way, the dew soaking my slippers and the ends of my dress.

46

I felt so...free.

The worst of times? Dick's wet lips and a tongue that tasted like an old ashtray. What came next was better. At least until the police showed up.

Mom's shrieking for me to come downstairs. Something about a missing pack of smokes. I'll finish later.

June 7

Dear Maggie

So that's why Mom's shipping me off. Again.

Hey, she should get an "A" for effort, right?

"It's just for the summer," Dad said when he dropped me off after that last dinner at The Steak Shack. (Remember when I told you about it, wink, wink). "Think of it as your writing retreat."

Yeah, yeah, Dad, I know. You've already explained it.

I can write my werewolf story without the distractions of my screaming bitchy mother or my fake friends calling my ugly pink phone. I can sit in the sun and write lofty thoughts in my juvenile yellow diary with the cheap lock.

Wish I'd never gone to prom. Then the police couldn't have busted the after-prom petting party.

When I say "police," I'm talking about Mom's poor relation cousin Bill Watts who works for the North Lyons police department.

He kept asking if I was fine, and then he took me to the station, where he kept dialing Mom until she woke up, so I could tell her I was fine.

All this concern for my fineness, but would anyone give me a cigarette? Nope. Not even when I asked very, very, very politely for one.

Bill Watts smoked, though, one cigarette after another.

Finally, after retelling my story a million times, Bill Watts brought me home where I had to listen to Mom yell at me for

hours about how I made her lose sleep over
me AGAIN!

Maggie, I did point out that if she'd
just shut her mouth, we'd both could've gone
to bed.

Which triggered more screeching and
frothing.

And a long-distance call to Dad to
get me out of her house until school starts if
he didn't want her to have a nervous
breakdown.

So now I have to spend the summer
in Dullsville.

All because I licked a penis.

June 8
Dear Maggie,

I don't know what to fucking pack.

I'm standing in the middle of my
room surrounded by piles of clothes, and I
don't even know what to fucking pack.

I know that Dad and Aunt Silly live in
a tiny house. But how tiny? My smallest

closet is bigger than my friends' bedrooms! And that's just for my shoes!

Fuck it. I'm calling Dad.

June 8

Dear Maggie,

So I called Dad.

He told me to keep it simple and bring a week's worth of writing clothes. And he told me not to bring my electric typewriter. He bought a new one for me.

"I was planning to surprise you, Mouse, but since you called…" Dad's voice trailed off, but I could hear the smile in it.

A brand-new typewriter. And he wants me to bring my "writing clothes."

God, I love my dad.

He has so much faith in me. So I just HAVE to write the world's greatest werewolf love story.

I can't let him down!!!!

June 8
Dear Maggie,

OK, so what the fuck are writing clothes???

Slacks? Capris? Plaid dresses with belts? Skirts and cardigans?

What the hell does Shirley Jackson wear when she writes???

Help!!!

June 8
Dear Maggie,

So I sorted out the piles and then rehung everything else back in the closets. I went with mostly capris, some slacks, one plaid dress with a belt and one skirt and cardigan.

And only a few pairs of shoes.

Some nightgowns, just in case.

June 9
Dear Maggie,

Well, I'm packed and ready to go.

I'm sitting on my bed with my suitcases at my feet, ready to start my prison sentence.

Mom just left the room. She had stood in the doorway, brandishing a cigarette with her newly manicured nails and reiterating for the one hundredth and forty-ninth time how I did it to myself and how this is for my own good.

I tell her to go fuck herself.

Finally she left.

Stomped to her room and slammed the door.

Probably to fuck herself.

June 9
Dear Maggie,

The drive to Shelby was uneventful.

Dad drove and didn't let me smoke.

I sat and looked out the window, not smoking, even though the windows were rolled down.

We passed some cities and stopped for gas and to pee.

We passed open fields full of thick grasses, daisies, black-eyed Susans, clover, Queen Anne's Lace, and the occasional dark cloud of insects.

We ate the peanut butter sandwiches and sugar cookies he brought for us to share.

When I got super bored, I brought out my color pencils and pad and sketched aconite.

"What are you drawing, Mouse?" Dad teased. "Werewolves."

I shook my head. "You have to guess."

Dad grinned. "No werewolves?"

"You have to guess."

Dad gave a sigh of pretend irritation. "Shoot, Mouse."

"It's something that's three feet tall. It has yellow-green stalks, teeny white eyes, purple hoods, and it's blue."

"A werewolf that's a Martian?" Dad asked, the corners of his eyes crinkling as he smiled.

I love my dad.

"No, Dad. Aconite."

"Aconite?"

"Yes, Dad. To kill, or, at the very least, subdue them."

He grinned, eyes on the road. "I can't wait to read it, Mouse."

"Not until it's published, Dad."

"I know."

I shut the sketchbook. No point in coloring anymore when I don't have one fucking sentence written to go with it.

Only good thing is that the air got cooler and sweeter the farther north we drove.

Finally we got to Shelby.

Only the two-story, L-shaped Shelby Motel looked modern. I saw a glimpse of tennis courts and a huge swimming pool as we passed the "Welcome to Shelby" sign.

More later. Bathroom's FINALLY free.

June 9

Dear Maggie,

Shelby's a lot different than North Lyons, but I figured you knew that.

It's a cutesy little tourist town full of adorable little A-framed shoppes with colorful cloth awnings and wooden signs hanging from wrought iron. There's soap shoppe and a candle shoppe and what looks like a head shoppe and jewelry shoppe and dippy clothes shoppes, you get the idea.

The roads on Front Street, where I saw all the shoppes are cobblestone. Figures.

"Where's the little men?" I asked Dad as we drove past the "Welcome to Shelby" sign.

He steered the car away from the cutesy-pie scene and into the neighborhoods. The shaded streets looked like checkerboards. Tall, boxy houses were mixed with tiny ones with gable roofs.

"Little men?" he asked.

"Yeah, little men in little green suits and peaked caps with tassels holding hands, skipping down the street, and singing, "Lalalalalalalalalala."

Dad ignored me. Can't blame him. After all, he's got to live in this syrupy place.

I tried again.

"You're right, Dad. Shelby's a great place to write the world's greatest werewolf love story."

Yeah, Dad wasn't going to bite.

You caught the sarcasm, right Maggie?

June 10
Dear Maggie,

Do you know the best ways to kill a werewolf?

Bloodletting.

Tearing off all four limbs. Slowly.

Peeling away its flesh with hot pincers.

Burning at the stake.

Religious education. Yeah, that's really a thing.

Decapitation.

Silver bullets.

And bringing it to Shelby for the summer.

Where it dies of boredom.

June 11

Dear Maggie,

I've been at Shelby two whole days. Guess how many words I've written?

For the werewolf story, I mean.

Yep. Zero. A big, fat, fucking ZERO.

I'm going to be eighteen in less than three months, AND my werewolf love story is going to die on the pyre of adulthood.

Fuck.

On the plus side, I like hanging out at Dad's office, and I like hanging out with Aunt Silly.

Her real name is Priscilla Matilda Rochelle. But everyone calls her Silly. Because she is. In a good way.

She wears these tent-like dresses in bright prints, like orange and green or yellow and magenta. She wears clay jewelry she makes herself: long beaded necklaces and dangly earrings off gold wires: hoops, bells, zebras, trout, spires, rutabagas. You name it, she probably has earrings that look like it.

She sells A LOT at the shoppes. Her most popular design is made from polished moonstones on silver wire. The shoppes sell them as fast as she stocks them. Aunt Silly said it's because the little tag she attaches to them.

This is what the tag says: *Moonstone (hecatolite) is named for Hecate, goddess of magic and the underworld. She waits for you at the crossroad. Bring your requests to her, for she sees the past, present, and future.*

The first day I helped her, Aunt Silly gave me a moonstone necklace for me to keep. The gem on my silver chain is round and bluish white, with splashes of gray, black, pink, and cobalt.

I immediately put it around my neck and clasped it. Aloud, I asked the goddess,

"Lead me to the world's greatest werewolf love story."

Aunt Silly bowed her head with the most reverent, "Amen." Then she grinned and reached for her smokes.

She wears scuffs around the house, and scarf on her curly blonde head, and she smokes like a bitch. She drinks pots of coffee and eats kid food: cold crunchy rainbow cereal and milk, peanut butter and jelly sandwiches, toaster pastries, and beanie weanies.

We eat with our bowls and plates on her lap because the kitchen table's full of her jewelry supplies. She only uses gems with "chatoyance," a new word for me. Not all gems have it. Gems with chatoyance have a slit of light in them that moves as you turn the gem. Cat eyes are like that, too. I wonder if werewolf eyes have it?

Aunt Silly keeps a transistor radio on her windowsill, and it's always tuned to the pop station. She will randomly get up and dance, with her hands stretched out and her hips swaying, like some tropical maiden in a grass skirt.

And she laughs. She laughs from sunup to sundown. And if she's not laughing, she's smiling. Aunt Silly is the most laid-back, easy-going, genuinely happy person I've ever met.

Even though her entire cottage could fit into my bedroom back home! And we share the space with colonies of dust bunnies. The walls are bare; the curtains are made from old bed sheets, which Aunt Silly takes down and washes every week.

Seriously, it's two tiny bedrooms on the east side of the house, a small kitchen and living on the west, and a bathroom in the middle. The sink is caked with months of soap and toothpaste.

I sleep in Dad's room; he sleeps on the sofa and only comes in the room for his clothes. This is how tight the room is. When he opens the drawers, they touch the foot of the bed.

My clothes live in my suitcase, which is fine with me, because Dad's room only had a little closet, and it's full of his clothes and Christmas decorations.

Getting to those clothes is a problem, too, because a beat-up old desk is blocking it. On that desk is my brand-new electric typewriter that Dad bought for me.

Anytime Dad wants something out of the closet, he has to unplug the typewriter and move the desk back and then squeeze into the space and slide the old bedsheet to one side.

Yeah, bedsheet. The dinky closets in this dinky house have no doors. Wait until you hear how we wash the clothes. Hint: it wasn't with a lint-free automatic washing machine and automatic dryer that automatically adjusts for fabric. In fact, if our housekeeper back in North Lyons thought she had something to bitch about (she didn't; she just bitched a lot), she should have done our laundry in Shelby.

Here's how we wash clothes here. Aunt Silly runs them through her wringer washer in the cellar, and I hang them on the line she has stretched between two old oaks.

The dishes, however, pile up everywhere until we run out. Then Aunt Silly reaches for her cigarettes and says, "Well, Carrie, I supposed we must."

And we do.

This is how it works.

First, I walk to the screened-in back porch for a bottle of white label, pink dish soap. The bottle in the kitchen is always empty, but she buys them by the case, and they live stacked against a wall inside the porch.

Then I run the water for five minutes to warm it up. Then I close the drain with a rubber plug on a chain, squirt a third of the thin liquid into the water, and watch it foam. When the sink is half full, I gingerly pick up any silverware I can find and drop them in, so the water can loosen the layers of hard gunk.

Then I turn off the water and play spades with Aunt Silly.

After a long, long while, I pull the plug and refill the sink. One of us washes, one of us dries. Then we repeat with the plates, and then the glasses, and so on.

Aunt Silly shares everything. Not just the chores.

She splits popsicles and sandwiches in half, the strawberry jelly dripping like blood onto my capris.

We sit cross-legged on the linoleum, each with our own spoon and the bucket of orange sherbet between us.

She never lights up without gesturing the pack of smokes in my direction.

She sets her hair with regular curlers, not electric ones. She pins mine with clips and then we smoke together.

Dad doesn't approve of the smoking, but he only says it with his eyes. Aunt Silly scolded the look.

"Fred," she said. "Better in here than out there."

He never said a thing, so I guess he couldn't argue with that!

June 12
Dear Maggie,

So my private bathroom back home has a sunken claw tub for soaking. I would pour half a bottle of Roses des Prés into the hot water as it filled, and the most heavenly aroma would fill the room.

I'd luxuriate in the bubbles as long as I wanted. If the water grew cold, I pulled the plug with my toes, turned the handle with my toes, and added more hot water, And then I'd push the plug back into the drain with my toes.

Here I share a water closet with Dad and Aunt Silly and shower with Aunt Silly's pink soap that smells like roses and golden baby shampoo, the cheapest shit you can buy in this town.

For a chick who digs color, she sure as fuck loves pink. The shower curtain is pink, the old round shag rug in front of the shower is pink, and all the towels are pink.

"What the fuck?" I asked her one day as I helped her fold a mountain of pink towels. I swear she let them pile up half a year.

"What the fuck what?" Aunt Silly asked.

"Why all the fucking pink? Pink is for plastic ballerinas in cheap jewelry boxes."

"And my mama."

So, Maggie, I forgot to tell you. Dad and Aunt Silly grew up in this fairy box. OK, I'm not going to tell you these towels are from their childhood because they're not.

But the last person who bought towels for this house was their mom, my grandma. I never met her, she died before I was born.

The only thing left of her are the pink rose bushes near the fence line. And hundreds of pink fucking towels.

This Christmas, I think I'll buy Aunt Silly some new towels. Some will be tangerine, and some will be lime.

I think she'll dig those, don't you?

June 11

Dear Maggie,

So far, the best thing about Shelby is hanging out with Dad. His Shelby office is a lot friendlier than his North Lyons office.

His North Lyons office is super big. He has five veterinarians working for him because Dad only works there when he visits me in North Lyons. He has technicians, a records gal, and two receptionists.

Everything is white and full of gleaming metal.

He has lots of exams rooms, surgical suites, an X-ray room, a lab, a separate wing for people to board their pets, and a spacious waiting area with plenty of room, even if fifty people with St. Bernard's all showed up at the same time.

Hell, the waiting room even as a mini waterfall. So, yeah, pretty exclusive shit. But Dad's got a lot of rich clients, even though North Lyons is pretty diverse as far as money goes: the haves, the sorta haves, the wishful haves, and the usual round of have nots.

The Shelby office on Front Street is a lot like the North Lyons office, EXCEPT it's MUCH smaller, and it doesn't have a waterfall. Dad's the only veterinarian, too. Shelby doesn't need more than one.

That's because it's just regular people who lives in Shelby most of the year, except during the summer and except from Thanksgiving weekend through the new year. Maggie, if you thought Aunt Silly sells a lot of shit now, you should come out during Christmas.

I'm getting all this second-hand, of course. But that's what Aunt Silly told me the other day as she showed me how make a wire loop on a bead so it can be threaded onto wire or hang from wire.

Aunt Silly's sales go down in the spring and fall, and she's happy about that. Because she works all spring and fall to make enough stock for the summer tourists and the Christmas tourists.

She told me that Shelby is transformed into a Christmas fairyland of soft glowing lights at night, mechanical displays, handcrafted items with an Old World flair, and even a fireworks show on the Saturday night before Christmas.

On St. Nicholas Day, the good saint himself rides into town on a horse drawn carriages and tosses chocolate wrapped in golden tinfoil out to his admirers.

On the Sunday before Christmas, eight reindeer pull Santa into town. He tosses out red and green suckers (appropriate) to the crowd.

Maggie, if you thought this place was overrun in the summer, it ain't nothin' compared to the Christmas season, Aunt Silly said.

So if I've got to be stuck here, better summer than winter, I guess.

I'll feel a lot better about my prison sentence AFTER I wrote the world's greatest werewolf love story!

June 11
Dear Maggie,

OK, here's why I like hanging out with Dad at his Shelby office.

So even though the outside looks like the candy witch cottage in Hansel and Gretel like all the shoppes here, the inside is WAY different, very modern. As I said, it's like his North Lyons office, except smaller.

Maggie, think of it like a carnival fun house. The outside is honeyed and coated in sugar, as fake as can be. The inside is where the real magic happens. With a head of science, a heart of love, and the gentlest hands you'd ever want to know, Dad turns fear into trust. He heals injuries and pain.

And when I'm not writing my werewolf story (which, unfortunately, is most of the time), and when I'm not helping Aunt Silly, I'm here at Dad's office, helping him with the animals.

I weigh animals and take their temperatures. I clean cages. I even help Dad do some basic charting and soothe animals that are scared or in pain as Dad treats them.

One day when Aunt Silly and I were nearly finished with our rounds, I saw a set of tiny, muddy tracks on the sidewalk. So I followed them. Sure enough, they led straight to Dad's office. I went inside, and he was wrapping a Pekinese's injured paw.

"Who's dog, Dad?" I asked.

Dad didn't look up because he was fastening the bandage. "I don't know yet, Caryn. The dog just wandered in here." Then he did look up and grin. "As I'm certain the owner will."

See? Even the dog instinctively knew the way to healing.

June 11

Dear Maggie,

My list of people I like has grown by one.

So now I like three whole people in the whole world, and all three of them live in Shelby.

Where I'm NOT writing a werewolf story.

Shit, Aunt Silly needs me. Be right back.

June 11

Dear Maggie,

OK, so this person I like works for Dad.

Her name is Wendy, and she's actually kinda sweet.

Wendy is part receptionist, part records person, part filing clerk, and part technician. Basically, Wendy does anything Dad needs that he can't do himself.

She's pretty in her own way although no one would look at her and think, "Wow!"

But she has this inner radiance that MAKES her look pretty.

Wendy is about as tall as me and maybe ten pounds heavier. She has a square, ruddy face and course, shoulder-length hair that she dyes blonde. She loves animals, and, like Aunt Silly, she is always happy, but she is not giddy happy.

She also wears one of Aunt Silly's rings. It's a large pale blue moonstone with pinkish undertones set in silver. She wears it on the index finger of her right hand.

Like I said, she has this radiance (maybe that's why her skin is ruddy) that just makes you feel good to be around her. Animals sense it, too. Maybe that's why Dad picked her to work for him.

I'd better watch it, Maggie, or I'll have a whole slew of people friends!

YUCK!

June 12
Dear Maggie,
Oh my fucking God!

Some guy came into Dad's office today with a blue-eyed, white Persian cat and the rottenest stink!

I felt bad for the cat, but when I called, "Here kitty, kitty," to get its attention, the cat ignored me. Dad said later that it's deaf. I'll bet it wished it couldn't smell either!

"Dad," I asked once the smelly guy left. "What the fuck was it?"

"Bergamot," Dad said as he wrote notes in the cat's chart. "People find its citrusy scent to be uplifting, energizing." He glanced up with teasing eyes. "What's the matter, Mouse? Too zesty for you?"

"He reeked like old floor cleaner that someone had pissed in. Maybe it WAS floor cleaner that..."

The office bell jangled, so I shut up, even before Dad gave me "that look."

Seriously, Maggie. He smelled so bad, even werewolves wouldn't soil their fangs on him!

June 13
Dear Maggie.,

Today I helped Aunt Silly deliver her orders. This was not as boring as it sounds.

Aunt Silly doesn't drive, and she doesn't own a car.

But she does own stacks and stacks of plastic containers with lids. She keeps them on the screened front porch.

And she still has Dad's old Liberty Coaster, parked on the porch until delivery day.

Aunt Silly takes orders at her "desk." She made it herself, from orange crates and a knobby piece of old plywood. She sits in her hard, molded plastic aquamarine chair (stolen from the set around the metal kitchen table) and takes orders when people call on her number 500 black Western Electric telephone.

When the phone rings, Aunt Silly rushes to her desk like it's God calling, grabs her number two pencil and yellow pad, and then jots the orders in a funny shorthand only she can read.

On delivery day, Aunt Silly brings pad and pencil to the kitchen table, as well as a black marker and masking tape. I stack towers of plastic containers and lids into Liberty Coaster and pull it into the kitchen.

Aunt Silly reads and ticks off the items; I pack the containers, label them in tape and marker, and arrange them in the wagon until it is full.

Then we pull the wagon to Front Street. We take turns pulling the wagon, giving each of us time to smoke. Aunt Silly whistled while she pulled.

Unlike F.P Rogers in North Lyons, a place so exclusive you need money just to breathe its name, much less peruse its fourteen floors of merchandise, most of the shoppes in Shelby specialize in just one item. Aunt Silly's jewelry is in most of them.

First stop: the candle shoppe.

The candle shoppe only sells hand-dipped or hand-poured candles of every hue and size. A waxy meld of vanilla, moss, and rose hangs in the air. A jumbled maze of wooden bins and freestanding wooden shelves holds the products.

I select a thick pine chunk with black flecks. It's called "The Forest at Midnight" and it smells of jasmine and sage, the way I imagine running through the woods at night on my werewolf's back.

The owner is also chunky, with dirty dishwater hair, muddy brown eyes, and a splotched, white apron. She looks as if she's butchered babies instead of mixing wax. She takes her products out of the containers and counts out a stack of bills for Aunt Silly.

Aunt Silly gives her the change from her little paisley coin purse.

I pay for my candle with Dad's bank card. He opened his wallet and gave it to me the first night after dinner.

I shook my head and pushed his hand away.

"I'm here to write Dad," I told him. "I can shop anytime in North Lyons."

But Dad insisted.

"I believe you will write the world's greatest werewolf story this summer, Mouse," Dad said. "I believe it with all my heart. And if you see an item that helps you write, I want you to buy it."

I accepted the card. Today, I bought my first item. This is another reason why I love my dad.

Then we went to the head shop (which is really an incense shoppe), the bath shoppe, the art shoppe, and a fucking ridiculous amount of clothing boutiques.

All the shoppes have wooden floors. Some are polished; some are scuffed and dusty; all are creaky.

It's weird how all these shoppes want her jewelry. But I guess they can't count on each tourist going into each shoppe.

I didn't give Aunt Silly any shit about helping her, either, until we turned onto Fourth Street, and I came face to face with the shoppe of my nightmares

"I'm going to Dad's," I told her. "My stomach hurts."

It really did, Maggie. I sprinted there just in time.

Must be all the fucking hamburgers.

June 13

Dear Maggie

I wasn't kidding about the hamburgers.

Aunt Silly isn't much for cooking. But she'll throw a frozen dinner in the oven or frozen burgers in a frying pan or no-label dogs in a pot of boiling water. Even I know how to make a salad or fry potatoes.

OK to be fair, so does Aunt Silly. But she hates it. So because she's so cool, I do it. She makes the meat, and I make a salad and fry potatoes.

Every single fucking night.

OK, on a couple nights, she made her special hamburger soup. Basically she thinned condensed tomato soup with milk and heated it in a pan while she fried the hamburger good and brown.

I watched the meat go from bloody to pink to sepia and wondered what raw flesh tastes like to a werewolf.

Once, I tried snatching a bite, and Aunt Silly slapped my hand and said, "Do you want tapeworms?"

"You're thinking of raw pork, Aunt Silly," I countered.

"Ohhhh, you're so fucking smart. Ever hear of a taenia saginata?"

"Nope."

"Well, that's a tapeworm that lives in undercooked beef, Miss Know-It-All."

"OK," I conceded.

Besides, I really didn't want to eat raw hamburger. So when I start writing the world's greatest werewolf love story, I'll just have to make that part up.

Then she pats the excess grease off the hamburgers, spoons the meat into the tomato soup, and then reheats it. Voila! Dinner is served.

In the morning, a thick layer of white fat, about an inch thick, lines the frying pan. Remember, we don't wash it until we need it again.

Breakfast is always the same, too: crunchy cold cereal. No strawberry crepes or Belgium waffles to ease the monotony.

For lunch, it's always peanut butter sandwiches with tall glasses of milk mixed with instant cocoa powder. But she does like fresh apples and oranges, so she keeps an old wooden bowl on the counter full of them.

When I get my first million-dollar royalty check, I'm hiring a fucking chef!

June 14

Dear Maggie,

So today I used Dad's bank card again to buy a pen and ink drawing of a unicorn by some local nut who tries to pawn his stuff onto the tourists, too.

He was sitting at a folding table on the sidewalk with a bunch of other artists. Everything sucked balls except for this unicorn. Probably the only sale these losers made all day.

I'm not sure how I'll use this unicorn in my werewolf story, but I'll figure it out...once I figure out what the story will be.

Now before you think I've gone all sugary and glittery, this isn't like the baby blue and pink unicorns that hold salt and pepper on Aunt Silly's counter. Nope. No glued-on eyelash fringe or golden horns, uh, uh.

This unicorn is one mean sonofabitch.

He's hairy and muscular like any galloping beast should be. His eyes are tantalizingly fierce, and his lips are curled back. A big fat maiden with a poofy night cap on her head is cradling him, but he looks ready to charge, a good thing, too, because that two-foot long spike on his forehead would come right out her mouth if rammed it you-know-where.

Is that why unicorns follow virgins?

June 14

Dear Maggie,

I forgot to tell you about this old cane Dad has hanging on the wall in his office.

It's made of mountain ash, which is also called rowan, remember? It's a beautiful golden brown cane, very knobby, with natural circles up and down its staff.

Next to it, Dad has a sign (What is it with Dad and Aunt Silly and their fucking notes and signs???) that a someone had stitched for him in red embroidery floss. It reads:

"Rowan-tree and red thread, hold the witches all in dread."

Dad said the druids in Scotland used to sing it. I knew that mountain ash is a protection against werewolves, but Dad said it's magic is protects against wishes and any kind of dark force.

I think it's funny that a magic protector of dark forces is displayed in Dad's office. Because Dad's office is anything but dark.

It's a large room that doubles as his library and an overflow for the storage room. He has a long bookcase filled with veterinary books, even his college textbooks, on the farthest wall.

He has cases of paper towel and puppy pads on one wall. One wall is bare, except for the cane and the sign.

Most people put their desks facing the door. But Dad's faces the window that looks out into a small yard. In fact, Dad has his desk close to the window, so he can watch the birds and the squirrels.

In fact, Dad had a bunch of feeders with different types of seed to attract different types of birds.

So far I have seen blue jays, chickadees, robins, cardinals, goldfinches, doves, sparrows, and even a woodpecker.

I love my dad.

June 15

Dear Maggie,

So I got the shit scared out of me today.

While hitting up some of the shoppes today, I saw it again, a shoppe that's straight out of my nightmares.

A clock shoppe.

Come on, Maggie, ask it. I can hear you anyway. What the fuck is so scary about a clock shoppe?

All right, I'll tell you. It's The Clock Man.

Ever since I was a kid, I've had this recurring nightmare about walking down a creepy street, all black and white and foggy like in some old horror flick. And I always stop at The Clock Shoppe.

In the dream, I'm already terrified, and I haven't even gone inside. But you know how dreams work. I have to go in; I have no choice. So I turn the handle on the dented metal door and inch inside.

The place is dim and dank and full of clocks, of course. But the faces on all these clocks have personalities, and they're not happy-go-lucky faces, either. They're sinister and murderous, and I edge away from them to the back of the room, where a curtain separates the main room from an even greater horror.

Suddenly the sheet whips aside, and The Clock Man stares down at me.

His face is round and pale like the Man in the Moon but without all its shadows. His hair is blond-gray and sparsely covers his scalp. His eyes are a blue-gray, more gray than blue. But the color was less important than what these eyes see.

He opens his mouth to speak...

...and then I wake up.

Now right before me was the clock shop, just like I dreamed it.

Maggie, I'm scared just to write it. I mean, why would I dream something I've never seen?

But then, maybe I have seen it. Maybe before Mom and Dad divorced, we visited Aunt Silly right here in Shelby, when I was a baby. Maybe this clock shop was already here. Maybe we went inside, and something scary jumped out.

That's the only explanation I've got.

Now, I have a question for you.

If the idea of a clock shop with a Clock Man frightens me, do you think it will frighten readers, too?

Good answer, Maggie. I think so, too.

Now why a werewolf story would have a clock shop with a Clock Man, I don't know.

I will have to give it some thought.

June 16
Dear Maggie,

Still thinking.

Not one blessed word of this werewolf story written yet.

I fucking hate my life.

June 16

Dear Maggie,

I came up with the best lines for The Clock Man (once I find a purpose for him in my story).

It's from "Paradise Lost" by John Milton. Remember it? We read it at North Lyons High last year.

Here are the lines:

"A mind not to be changed by place or time.
"The mind is its own place, and in itself
"Can make a heav'n of hell, a hell of heav'n."

And I want to use some kind of implication that if the main character doesn't heed his warnings, she will become trapped in time.

Isn't that great?

Now I just have to write the damn book.

June 17

Dear Maggie,

Last night as I shut my bedroom door, Dad came out of the bathroom. And he said, "Good night, and don't let the werewolves bite."

He laughed and asked, "Remember, Mouse?"

Actually, I had forgotten until that moment. But Dad used to say it all the time when he tucked me into bed at night, when he still used to hug and kiss me.

"Good night! Don't let the werewolves bite," he'd say and bare his teeth and lean toward my forehead.

I'd squirm and squeal, knowing only a kiss was coming. Then I'd put my arms around his neck in a werewolf hug.

"I love you, Dad," I'd say.

"I'd love you, too Mouse," he'd say back.

And then he'd switch the light off and shut the door all the way. Even when I was little, I wasn't afraid of the dark. I'd just lay

88

there and think about werewolves. The next thing I knew, it was morning.

If I had a super tense day with Mom and couldn't sleep, Dad would tell me to count werewolves instead of sheep. Dad used to sing me lots of fun songs, too. Here's one:

"Oh where, oh where
"Has my little dog gone?
"Oh where, oh where can he be?
"With his ears cut short
"And his tail cut long
"Oh where, oh where can he be?"

And Dad always read bedtime stories to me that had wolves in them: "The Three Little Pigs," "Little Red Riding Hood," "The Wolf and the Fox," "The Wolf and the Seven Young Kids," "The Boy Who Cried Wolf," "The Wolf in Sheep's Clothing," "The Dog and the Wolf," "The Wolf and the Crane," "The Wolf and the Lamb," "The Mother and the Wolf," "The Wolf and the Kid," "The Kid and the Wolf," "The Shepherd Boy and the

Wolf," "The Wolf and His Shadow," "The Wolf and the Sheep," "The Wolf and the Lion," "The Wolf and the Lean Dog," "The Wolf and the Ass," "The Wolf and the Goat," "The Wolf and the Shepherd," "The Wolves and the Sheep;" "The Stag, the Sheep, and the Wolf;" and "The Wolf, the Kid, and the Goat."

Long after they split up, and long after Dad said I was too old for kisses from him, I'd call Dad on my princess phone at two o'clock in the morning just to bitch. He'd always pick up, sleep slurring his voice, and just be my dad.

When he'd start to snore, he'd wake himself up and say, "Mouse, have you tried counting werewolves?"

I love my dad.

June 18
Dear Maggie,

Despite being an oasis for dippy tourists, Shelby has no night life, unless that's what you call sitting in the backyard with Dad and Aunt Silly.

Because Dad is such a great veterinarian, he usually doesn't come home until late. Sometimes he eats cold hot dogs or warmed-up hamburgers and fried potatoes, but lots of times he's already had dinner — Wendy gets takeout from one of the cafes and brings it right to his office.

Dad isn't much for talking, but he does like company. Usually by the time he comes home, Aunt Silly and I are sitting on wicker chairs in the screened back porch, where the mosquitoes can't get us.

We're watching lightning bugs and listening to the music of cicadas while we smoke. Sometimes we're planning our day for tomorrow, how many orders to fill or what shoppes need refills.

But usually we're talking about nothing. Aunt Silly is good at that. She knows a lot about a little, and she likes to ramble. She's a walking, talking encyclopedia, and she thinks most of it is funny.

No, Maggie, I can't think of any examples. That's not the point of this entry.

Then what's the point, you say? I'm trying to tell you. This time of the day, when Dad comes home and Aunt Silly and I are sitting in the June night with a screen to separate us from biting creatures that leave itchy welts is the most magical time of the day.

Dad greets us pleasantly, "Hi, Prissy. Hi, Mouse. Did you have a nice day?"

We say yes, and then add something bland like, "I sold two hundred dollars of moonstone necklaces today" or "I typed a hundred words and ripped it all to fucking shreds."

Then Dad says, "Great job, Prissy" and "You'll get it, Mouse. You still have all summer."

Then Aunt Silly says, "How was your day, Fred?"

And Dad always says, "I'm blessed."

Then he sits down and takes out his pipe and lights it. We all sit quietly together, Dad smoking, Aunt Silly rocking, and me hunched on the wicker chair with my knees to my chin, reveling in the sounds of the night and the creak of the old wood and the smell of tobacco, a robust and fragrant smell that's hard to describe except that it smells like a hunt at night.

For all of Dad's objections about the stink of cigarette, he does like to smoke a pipe at night. It's the only time he ever smokes it. I guess it's like how some people like to drink after work. But Dad doesn't drink at all, not even a cold beer on a hot day.

After a while, I start feeling sleepy, a relaxed floaty feeling that feels almost like flying. Dad and Aunt Silly will murmur to each other. I guess it's their way of having a private conversation without telling me to get lost.

That's fair; after all, they've been brother and sister longer than Dad's been my dad. And Aunt Silly never married, and Dad's been divorced so long that they've lived together more than they haven't.

June 19
Dare Maggie,

You know, I realized something today. Aunt Silly and I are not just related.

We're bonded in the spirit.

I was helping her load her orders not the wagon when my eye caught one of the moonstones, glowing with, of all the fucking things, pink undertones in the sunlight, not just hints like my necklace.

Still...Aunt Silly works with moonstones. I write creatures who love the moon.

And now I also wonder if we are somehow connected through pink. Ick!

June 19

Dear Maggie,

So tonight while we were smoking and waiting for Dad to come home, I asked Aunt Silly about her mom liked pink.

She just laughed and said that my question was ridiculous.

"Why doesn't anyone like a color, Caryn?" she countered.

"I'll bet yours isn't pink," I joked.

Aunt Silly took a hard drag and blew it out. "Nope."

"Then what?" I persisted.

"All of them," she answered. "All of them except pink. Although," and here she took another drag, less hard, more like a little suck and way more reflective, "I can tolerate hot pink. But it's gotta be super bright and glossy."

She grinned at me, and I grinned back at her.

June 20

Dear Maggie,

I fucking hate Shelby and its crowd of nouveau riche tourists. They probably save all year just to come here and walk the streets with their smug looks as if they're doing everyone a favor.

The only good thing is that they also bring their Yorkies and poodles and the "air" here doesn't agree with them. So they bring them to Dad's office for pampering. The dogs probably act sick on purpose, just to get away from these snooty bitches.

And Dad just kisses their asses.

I feel like telling them that Dad doesn't need their next month's mortgage payments and their kids' college tuition. He has two offices, including the one in North Lyons that's so exclusive they can't afford to traipse through its doors.

But I don't. Dad wouldn't like it, and I don't want to disappoint Dad ever.

Besides, once the owners are gone for the day, the real fun begins. I'm able to calm their frantic yipping with just a few soothing words and gentle pats, so Dad can get their vitals and examine them.

One little blue and brown Yorkie today practically quivered with terror as it held my gaze with its shoe button eyes and yipped in a quiet whiny way. By the time Dad was removing the thorn from its red, swollen paw, it was wagging its tail and licking the back of my hand. You could see the smile in its eyes!

On those rare occasions something really is wrong with these pups, it's all the owner's fault.

One dumb cunt actually told Dad today, "He was fine until he ate the ice cream cone we bought him."

Ice cream? For a Dachshund?

Dad needed to take his rowan cane off the wall and beat that owner bloody!

June 20
Dear Maggie,

There are just two times I can tolerate Shelby, well, three.

I do like hanging out with Dad at his office. I do like hanging out with Wendy. And I do like hanging out with Aunt Silly.

But nighttime in Shelby has its own kind of magic.

When I'm home (North Lyons home, not Dad's and Aunt Silly's home), the walls are so thick and the ceilings so high, it's almost like being in a soundproofed box. You can't hear the hum of the central heating or cooling; you can't even hear the sound of the water softener when it starts up in the middle of the night.

And since I had my own private room and bath on the other side of the second floor, far, far away from Mom, I couldn't hear her run water for a bath or shower. She never woke me up in the middle of the night with her drunken puking or peeing.

But here, in this dinky house with walls as thin as corrugated paper, I hear every sound in the night so clearly, it's like I'm a werewolf prowling outside at night.

I hear the murmuring of voices and the chirring of insects and, every now and then, the distant rumble of cars.

Because I sleep in Dad's room in the back of the house, I have windows on two sides the side by my bed and directly across from me, which looks out into the backyard.

So I leave those curtains open at night and lay across my bed, covers off because this room is so fucking hot without air conditioning (even with the box fan set to "high"), and pretend I'm a werewolf bathing in the moonlight.

I pretend this even when there's not a moon.

I'd lie here naked if I was sure no one would walk in. But the door doesn't have a lock. And the old wood is so warped, it won't close all the way.

Unfortunately, because my room is also by the bathroom, I DO hear Aunt Silly and Dad when they get up for their middle-of-the night leaks. What the fuck is it with old people that they can't hold their water for eight fucking hours?

Usually it's Aunt Silly who gets up first. She wakes me up when she drops the lid, It goes off like a bomb, and I jolt awake, nearly exploding out of my skin!

By the time my heart calms down, and I'm drifting off to sleep, Dad's in there, sounding like a roaring waterfall. Like the sound an elephant would make if he was suspended twenty feet in the air and was denied potty privileges for a day!

I fold the pillow over my head and glower in the dark at the numbers on the little clock, its glowing green phosphorescence staring back at me like a cyclops werewolf.

And then, because my dad is a doctor and does all the right shit even in the middle of the night and when he's half asleep, he carefully washes his hands for a full thirty seconds. And he runs the water at full blast!

And they wonder why I'm cranky in the morning!

June 21
Dear Maggie,

Speaking of the middle of the night rudeness of old people, I have to tell you about my Dad's one quirk.

He has to close everything. And by everything, I mean fucking everything!

He always puts both lids down on the toilet. He always shuts every door and drawer all the way; not even a sliver of a crack can be left open. Drawers especially drive him nuts. He can't stand to see them ajar.

"It's either opened or its closed, Caryn," he used to tell me when I was a kid, and he'd lecture me about the proper way to push a drawer into place. "You can't have it both ways. Pandora didn't just "sort of" open the box."

There's a reason why Dad would reference Pandora's box, Maggie. More on this later.

If Dad is packing a box, he carefully folds the flaps, so they lay perfectly flat. Curtains are either open or closed, no partway for him.

He even waits for the tiny "click" on the metal medicine cabinet whenever he grabs an aspirin or bicarbonate of soda or ointment for the pain in his leg, a leftover pain, Aunt Silly told me, from a dog that bit him years ago.

That was back when he and Mom were still married, and I was a baby. On days his leg really acts up, he walks with a cane, the rowan cane that hangs in his office. His leg aches, some, all the time, but it really throbs when the moon is full.

Since Dad is all obsessed with closing shit, I had to ask Aunt Silly why he doesn't fix my fucking door.

But she only shrugged, reached for the matches, and told me that, when I wasn't here and Dad slept in his own bed, he'd just leave the door wide open all night.

See what I mean? No halfway for him!

I guess that also means an animal is sick or well. And if an animal is sick, Dad works very, very hard to make that animal ALL better.

So, yeah, I close every drawer. Because I love my dad.

June 22
Dear Maggie,

OK, so you know the story of Pandora's box, right?

You don't? Well, what the fuck. All right, here goes.

The story is from Greek mythology. It starts with Prometheus, the god who created people out of clay and gave them light by stealing fire from heaven.

Well that pissed off Zeus. He's the king of all the gods. So he decided to get even. He had another god created Pandora out of the earth. In the meantime, Prometheus doesn't trust Zeus and warns his brother Prometheus to refuse any gift Zeus might give him. But you know guys when they see a pretty girl.

Zeus shows up with Pandra, who was made out of the earth. She's carrying a jar, also made from the earth (it later becomes a box). Epimetheus totally ignores his brother's advice, and Pandora opens up her jar and lets out famine, sickness, death, envy, hate, writers block...every kind of evil that's now in the world.

All that was left inside the box was hope.

Back when I was little, so little I can't remember the first time, Dad used to call any inspiration I had for any idea my Pandora's Box.

"You just open your box and all these ideas come flying out," Dad used to caution me. "But all the ideas are not good ideas. Sometimes you have to let the bad ones fly away so you can let the good one out."

That's one reason why I haven't written my werewolf love story yet. All the idea I've had are bad ones. All the stories I've started are bad ones.

Hell, I've taken that stupid box and shaken it upside down and peered into all its dark corners. If that one good idea is in there, it's hiding pretty damn good.

So now I don't know what to do.

But I like to think it IS in there, trapped somewhere, and begging me to let it out. Just thinking about it makes me, smile.

"Let me out, Caryn," my one teeny, little good idea begs from somewhere tucked away. "Let me out! Let me out!"

I know what you're thinking, Maggie. Maybe the idea just needs to grow bigger so I can see it.

But the way I've fed it on werewolf thoughts, werewolf lore, werewolf stories, werewolf research, and shitty first drafts, the fucking idea should be as big as Porphyrion.

June 23
Dear Maggie,

So today I got to bathe a stray.

His hair was scraggly and long and dirty and matted, even the hair on his ears. Someone found him whimpering on the side of the road near the grassy fields between Thornton and Shelby and brought him into Dad.

So after Wendy fed him, Dad gave him a quick exam to make sure nothing was broken and then he had to stitch up a cat with a torn earn. So he asked me to give the poor little homeless pup a bath.

I've given lots of dogs their baths. So I knew what to do.

First, I set the dog on the floor and brushed out his matted fur. That makes it easier to get the dog clean. Also, the matted parts will hang onto the water and make the dog's skin all itchy and rashy. He whimpered a lot, but I murmured and cooed to him to calm him and let him know he was safe me. He must have understood because he stopped whimpering. And he did not squirm or try to run away.

Then I filled the deep tub with lukewarm water. Hot water will burn a dog's skin. Then I picked up this bundle of hair and set him in the water. He started to whimper again, but I patted him in a soothing way until he settled down. Then I lathered up a special dog shampoo dog and worked it through his fur. Human shampoo can dry out a dog's skin.

But I didn't just suds him up and rinse him. I gave him a nice massage, too, starting at the top of his head and working my way to the base of his tail. I felt all his muscles relax as my hands and tips of my fingers gently kneaded his muscles. Then I rinsed away the suds, the dirt, and the last of his trepidations. He was actually smiling and wagging his tail by the time I started rubbing him dry with a white (not pink!) fluffy towel.

"Good doggy," I told him over and over. "Good doggy."

Dad came in just as I patted away the last drips. He smiled, too.

"Well, Caryn, you sure have a way with animals," Dad said.

His praise made me feel warm and tingly to the roots of my hair!

If I do have a way with animals, Maggie, it's all because of Dad!

June 24
Dear Maggie,

Brought home a great find today, and I didn't have to waste Dad's money on it, either.

While Aunt Silly was haggling with the owner of one of the antique shoppes, I wandered the dusty store, peering into old orange crates full of junk and letting my eyes roam over the knickknacks on the shelves.

I found it in a cardboard box of junk on the windowsill. It was a long rusty key like you see in old scary movies. It had a flower with five petals at its base and metal vines twisting over its length. When I picked it up, I felt its weight.

I held it up and called, "How much for the key?"

The shoppe keeper, hot and harried, just shrugged.

"Just take it," he said.

So I slipped it into the pocket of my capris and mused on the secrets it might unlock in my werewolf story.

Once I come up with some, that is!

June 25
Dear Maggie,

Today an amazing thing happened.

I walked into Dad's office today in time to see Wendy write a receipt for a very familiar-looking man.

So I asked him, "Dad, who was that man?"

But Dad kept writing. His brow was furrowed, and his lips were slightly pursed, signs he did not hear me.

"Dad," I said louder. "Who was that man?"

He clicked the pen shut and slid it into his lab pocket. "Man?"

I followed him out the room. He set the chart on Wendy's desk.

"The one who paid his bill this morning for the house call."

"Oh," he said. "That's Gordon James. One of my clients."

Huh? *Gordon James?*

"Gordon James?" I echoed, confused.

"Yes," Dad said.

"Oh."

"You sound disappointed, Mouse," Dad teased as he headed to the next exam room. "Were you expecting someone else?"

"I thought it was Randolph Monroe McCallister St. Martin."

A proud look. A gentle smile. Like the time I won the science fair for my hamster project.

Then Dad reached for the chart from the clear plastic holder screwed into the door.

"You did?" But he was already scanning the lines.

"Yes," I said. "He's older, of course, and his hair is falling out. His belly hangs over his belt a little, too. But the look is there, especially in his eyes.

"You're as keen as a bloodhound," Dad said. "But this time you are off the scent. The man really is Gordon James, president of First Bank of Shelby."

"Or it's really Monroe, hiding out and lying."

"He's Shelby born and raised, just like me, just like your Aunt Silly."

Well, what the fuck?

Dad opened the door. "Coming, Mouse?"

I shook my head. "Gotta go, Dad. Inspiration is calling."

I hated lying to Dad, but I needed to think.

So after Dad went into the exam room, I lit up and headed outside.

Dad would never lie, especially to me.

But Gordon James' resemblance to Monroe really bugged me.

And the fact I cared bugged me even more.

June 26
Dear Maggie,

And so I followed him.

I was stacking cat litter when Gordon James came into the office to make an appointment for a house call.

Why all the house calls, I wondered. What was he raising that he couldn't bring into the office, a mountain lion?

I had to know.

And so, in the sweltering, midday, Shelby sun, which the cloth awnings did little to deflect, I followed him.

I made an excuse about hurrying home to help Aunt Silly with...something. I got out of Dad's office good and fast and followed him.

Closely, but not too closely, I kept him in view as I slunk down First Street.

Dad's just mistaken, I told myself. Or maybe he doesn't realize who Gordon James really is. Maybe Monroe killed the real Gordon James, hypnotized the town, and stole Gordon's identity.

Won't he pay when the truth comes out?

Every now and then Monroe paused, as if listening. But I was quicker than he. He never saw me flattened between two buildings. Or perhaps he only observed an innocent girl, hands clasped behind her back, admiring the hand-dipped candles in the windows.

Go ahead, I scoffed to myself. Look around. Be clever. I'm as stealthy as a werewolf, as silent as a shadow.

Yes, that's right. I'm a shadow, the shadow of unease. You won't see me. And if you do see me, you won't catch me.

Idiot. What a fucking idiot.

The trail ended at a large, three-story brick building at the end of First Street. He turned the corner and walked to the rear. I waited and waited, but he never came out, so I'm guessing he had important business there.

Or lived there.

In hiding.

June 26
Dear Maggie,

So it turns out the tall building is a bank.

"Take this to the bank for me, Mouse," Dad said when I popped back in.

He handed me a blue vinyl bag. It looked like a pencil case, only a little larger.

"Sure Dad," I told him. "Where's the bank?"

Dad looked up. He looked surprised.

"Tall brick building at the end of the street," Dad said. "You can't miss it."

OK, I didn't miss the tall building at the end of the street. But I HAD missed the sign on the front because I was too busy stalking my prey. Sure enough, it read, "First Bank of Shelby."

It's still Monroe, I thought as I handed the blue bag to the teller and waited for her to write a receipt. It's still Monroe, pretending to be Gordon James Bank President when he's really hiding something.

Maybe the teller is pretending, too. She's about Mom's age, but with wrinkles. She'd have to know who he is.

"Here's your receipt," the liar said as she slid the paper under the glass. "You're Caryn, Dr. Rochelle's daughter?"

I'm not fooled, you lying cunt. But two can play this game.

"Yes." I smiled back at her. "I'm spending the summer here."

"I hope you have a great summer," she added.

"I'm having a wonderful summer," I choked out.

I was only nice to her because of Dad. Because he has to live and work here.

And because I didn't want her to know I was onto her — and Monroe.

Maggie, I swear, I'll find out his secret. And then I'm going to expose the bastard.

I wonder if there's a reward?

June 27
Dear Maggie,

You should see these two old-ass books I bought yesterday. One is <u>Mother Goose Rhymes</u> from 1912, and it's nothing like the Mother Goose book Dad used to read to me.

The cover says it has fifty full page black illustrations. They look like the cover, which looks like a silhouette.

On the cover is Mother Goose herself, except she reminds me of a Wicked Witch. She's riding a silhouette of a goose and urging it on with her riding crop. At the top left corner is a silhouette quill pen and in the bottom left corner is a gaggle of white marching geese against the black.

This version has lots of rhymes that don't make it into kids' books today. Like this one:

"Hink minx! the old witch winks,
"The fat begins to fry:
"There's nobody home but jumping Joan,
"Father, Mother, and I."

The other book is called <u>Folk Tales of Old England</u>. It has a cloth cover and yellowed pages that are surprising sturdy since the book is warped from water damage.

I flipped through it last night in bed. One story really appealed to me. It's called "The Green Lady" and it's about a young girl who asks her father for a cake and a bottle of beer (yech!) because she's going out into the big, wide world to seek her fortune.

Well, the father is hungry, too, so he persuades her to share the meager dinner. Afterwards, he sends her to an old, abandoned cottage in the woods. He told her that if she knocks on the door, the Green Lady who lives there will give her work.

So the Green Lady does. The Green Lady tells the girl to work hard and never look through the keyhole. Of course, the girl does just that. She sees the Green Lady dancing with a bogeyman.

This pisses off the Green Lady (I mean, she did warn the girl). After giving her three more chances, she gouges out the girl's eyes and kicks her out of the cottage with a tied up bundle.

As the girl wanders around, she stumbles into a young man sitting at the edge of a well. He told her the fishes (I'll come back to this) sent him to help her. The man tells her to wash her eyes in the well

(Why he didn't help her and how she didn't fall in, being blind, isn't explained in the story).

After she washes her eyes, she can see. Then she opens the bundle, and it's full of money. The man marries her (probably for her money), and they "live happily ever after).

The part I really like is the part about the fishes. The Green Lady sends the girl to the well to get some fish for her. Eventually the girl pulls out three silver fish. Each time, she pulls out a fish, the fish tells her:

"Wash me, and comb me,
"And lay me down softly,
"And lay me on a bank to dry,
"That I may look pretty,
"When somebody comes by."

I think this is a strange rhyme for fishes to say, which only proves the writer was probably smoking a hookah with the caterpillar on Lewis Carroll's magic mushroom.

But WHAT IF...

What if a werewolf said those lines? And what if the "somebody" who comes by is his true love?

Damn, Maggie! Why can't I write this story???

June 28
Dear Maggie,

Dad worked late tonight, and I helped him.

Nothing special, just run of the mill illnesses.

But Dad had left in the middle of the day.

I had sat in front of the typewriter all morning, nothing coming but a few dumb phrases.

Restless and cranky and crampy, I wandered to Front Street to see Dad.

"House call," Wendy said when I stopped in.

You heard that right, Maggie! If an animal is super sick or hurt, Dad goes to it. I love him so much.

He was gone a long time, a couple hours, maybe. In the meantime, I filed some reports and cleaned a couple cages.

Dad looked surprised to see me, but he didn't ask.

When the last patient left, it was dark.

Dad said, "Thank you for your help today, Mouse."

And I said, "You're welcome, Dad."

Then he walked through all the rooms and drew the blinds and latched the shutters.

I knew why, but I asked anyway. The first time I saw Dad do this was back in North Lyons, when I was little.

"Are they afraid of the dark?" I had asked.

"It's the full moon," Dad said. "The animals get agitated."

I loved this!!!!

"Because they're werewolves?"

I did half-hope that was the reason.

But Dad looked grave. "Because they're nocturnal. They want to hunt."

Since then, I've learned a lot about lunar cycles and circadian rhythms from Dad.

Oysters close up their shells during a full moon.

Rattlesnakes hide during a full moon so other animals don't eat them. Badgers won't mark their territory.

Doodlebugs dig larger sand pits during a full moon to trap ants.

"We'll be busy tomorrow, Mouse," Dad said with a weary sigh as he turned off the last light.

I knew why. The full moon lures nocturnal predators, like the dogs and cats of Shelby, out of their houses in easy search of prey with the moon's bright light.

More roaming pets mean more injuries: abrasions, sprains, breaks.

It also means more owners will get bit in pursuit of their runaway pets. But that's not our problem. We only treat the pets.

"If I'm free, Dad, I'll help," I promised.

Because who knows? May be THIS full moon will unleash my creative energy?

If not, I'll be howling.

Get it?

June 28

Dear Maggie,

So I have this disorder during my "time of month." It's another reason why I relate to werewolves.

I always "start" when the moon is full.

That is the one hundred percent truth, cross my heart.

But the symptoms start before that. As the moon swells, I swell. Like I have to take off my rings, and my fingers are too stiff to hold a pen. My shoes pinch, and so do my dungarees and capris.

My head hurts and I don't want to write. Like Dad's patients, I get agitated, but the only thing I want to hunt and eat is chocolate. I get super sleepy during the day but can't fall asleep at night.

When I can't sleep, I'll howl at the full moon. This causes Mom to flip, which is why I do it. I tried it out tonight on Aunt Silly, and she just laughed.

So I did it again, a really loud, full-throated howl. She laughed so hard she peed herself. I laughed as she threw her pee-soaked scuffs away and waddled off for the mop. So did she. Which leaked more pee.

As the moon recedes, so do I. The headache goes away, and my creativity returns.

But tonight the moon is high in the sky. Tonight werewolf fangs drip, and so do I.

Good stuff, huh?

June 29
Dear Maggie.

Well, I dripped all right.

I went out for a smoke and a walk around the block after dinner to try to force the thoughts out, and I got caught in the rain!

I knew a storm was brewing. The sky had darkened, and the air smelled like rain. But I wasn't going far, just to the next street.

Well, once I reached the street, the air cooled, and the wind picked up. So I hurried up with my cigarette but not fast enough. Just three houses from Aunt Silly, and I get caught in a downpour!

I tried to run and twisted my knee. Aunt Silly iced it right away, so it's not too swollen. I mean, I can walk without limping. I can't even borrow Dad's rowan cane now that the moon is full because he's using it.

I wanted inspiration, not to get soaking wet. Am I asking for too fucking much?

June 29

Dear Maggie,

I'm so fucking restless and frustrated, I can't stand it!

So I left.

Right after everyone went to bed, I left the house and just...walked.

Up and down the streets of this quiet, boring neighborhood with the full golden moon I walked on my slightly swollen knee. I walked slowly, so I wouldn't slip, fall, and really fuck it up. Then I'd have to crawl home!

Still, it smelled so good outside, all muddy and grassy. I squatted down to touch the slick grass. Could a werewolf run over slippery grass after a rain? I closed my eyes and rubbed my hand over the grass, trying to experience it from the paws of a werewolf.

Part of the reason I like to walk the neighborhoods is the hill. It's way off in the distance, beyond all the houses. It's the perfect hill for a werewolf...and too fucking faraway for me to reach foot.

But if I was a werewolf, I would head for this hill. Maybe I can add it to my story. It's a purplish blue in the distance, but I'm imaging lots of lush grass. In fact, the moon comes to rest almost at its highest point. It's just so...werewolf-like.

And then, Maggie, I think, "What's the use?"

June is nearly done, and I have not written one fucking, god-blessed word!

June 30
Dear Maggie,

OK, this is a long ass entry, so pay attention.

The most wonderful thing happened to me today. I'm so excited, I'm shaking.

But it happened, Maggie. It really, really, really happened.

And the best part about this whole experience, other than it happened, is the unexpectedness of it. It finally happened! It happened on the last day of the month, and I didn't have to force it.

Yeah, yeah, I know Maggie. I'm getting to it.

But I do have to say, Dad was right. He was totally, completely, absolutely, one hundred percent right that Shelby was the best place in the whole wide world to write the world's greatest werewolf love story.

How do I know this? Because I wrote chapter one today. I have a title for the book.

And it's all because the inspiration for the story was right here in Shelby.

OK, so here's what happened.

Wendy didn't come to work yesterday or today.

Summer cold, Dad said. And an earache.

I found out after lunch.

Aunt Silly settled at the table to make jewelry. I went to my room not to write a werewolf story.

What a wasted summer, I told myself. What a wasted life.

Eighteen was around the corner, and I hadn't written the world's greatest werewolf story.

Why wouldn't the fucking words come?

"I'm going for a walk," I told Aunt Silly.

"Take two," she said, holding out the pack.

I did...and a book of matches from the counter.

And I walked. Up and down, through and around, I walked.

I sucked the smoke in and wished I could blow the words out. What the actual fuck was wrong with me?

Shelby afternoons, at least in the neighborhoods, are typically quiet. The brats are napping, and the mothers, if they're outside, are squatting in the yard plucking weeds or slouched in a lawn chair with a dime store novel and glass of iced tea.

Front Street has more bustle because of all the tourists milling in and out of the shoppes. It's easy to spot the tourists and not just because they're annoyingly loud.

The men wear baggy pleated trousers and striped shirts and stroll, hands in pockets, alongside their wives; they look relaxed or bored, except when they're eyeballing a tanned set of young legs in shorts.

Most of the women wear belted pleated skirts and collared shirts with two buttons at the top. They clutch leather handbags, and their rhinestone sunglasses sparkle in the sun.

Everyone smells of chlorine and suntan oil.

But it's their money that makes this ho-hum town go 'round. Yay.

Somehow, my steps led me to Dad's office. I took a couple of last drags and crushed the cigarette under my toe, wishing I could press the story out of my mind as easily.

Then I went inside to cuddle the kittens.

There's three of them in the back room, all vying for my attention by swiping their paws across the cage and mewing in excited little squeaks.

I shut the door, lift the latch, and drop, cross-legged, to the cold tile, as they scamper out and swarm onto my lap. I've already named them.

The little calico is Tiger. The tuxedo is Penguin. The tortoiseshell is Alderman Ptolemy Tortoise.

I nuzzle Penguin, his soft fur melts into my cheek. Ptolemy climbs up my back. Tiger rubs her cheek against my arm and purrs.

I'm happy and calm.

After long, long while, the kittens tire of the cuddles. They shake off my scent and lick away the rest, little rough pink tongues smoothing back their ruffled fur.

Gently, I placed them back into the cage and fastened the door.

I washed my hands with soap that smells like bubblegum and used the wet paper towel to de-fur my blouse.

Dad is in his office, leaning back in his swivel chair, and murmuring into the telephone. I wandered to the waiting room and saw the pile of files waiting for Wendy. She likes animals, too, so I've grudgingly decided she's not a horrible human being and probably legitimately sick.

Besides, putting away the files helps Dad, too.

I'd only replaced three into their gray steel drawers when I had the idea.

I craned my neck to be sure Dad was still on the phone.

Then I opened the drawer marked F to J and quickly flip through the manila folders, skimming the white tabs, until I came to **GORDON JAMES**.

I held its place with a finger, pulled it, out, and flipped it open: 666 Fifth Street.

What the fuck?

I swiftly slid the folder back into its place and filed the rest of the stack. Then I ripped off a piece of paper from the yellow pad and scrawled a note to Dad so he knew I was the brownie.

Then I sped out the door to Fifth Street.

Like the other houses in Shelby, this tall boxy house had plenty of shade from all the old, gnarled trees. But only Gordon James's was full of rowan trees and tall, thick hedges.

Rowan.

Just like Dad's walking stick.

Fucking copycat.

I looked left and right. The street was deserted. I sidled to the side and scanned for nosey people and an opening in the edge.

I saw no people.

But I did find an opening,

Forgetting about my sore knee, I dropped, stopped, and yelped! Way to Go, Caryn, I told myself. Why not just a megaphone and announce your arrival to Gordon James?

I sat back on my haunches for a moment, pressing my hands over my knee to soothe the sting. Then I started crawling through the prickly patch and among the trees, gingerly, but like a bloodhound, head down, sniffing for I didn't know what. I only smelled sweet timothy grass and earthy dirt, stuff you'd expect to smell when your face is that close to someone's yard.

My eyes remained sharp for intruders, my ears tense for their sounds.

I easily remained hidden.

I inched my way to the back of the house, even more thickly sown with trees, and debated the best way to discern his secrets.

Should I crouch behind one of the mountain ashes and trail him when he leaves? Or should I look for a way into the house and find out his secrets for myself?

One rowan bade me to look up, so I did.

Its branches stretched far out, like spokes on a large beach umbrella, spokes that nearly touched the attic window, which was opened for air.

I could shinny up one tree, crawl across a thick branch like a stealthy cat, and bam! Into the house I'd go!

But as I assessed the strength of the branch, I noticed how slender it was away from the tree. Would it bear my weight?

Maybe?

And then I remembered my sore knee? What if I pressed too hard on it and lost my balance?

I headed for the basement windows, over ground as fake as people.

A few minutes ago, on the sidewalk, studying the lush expanse, and plotting my strategy, the yard looked soft and manicured, a pleasant place to lounge.

Down close is the truth.

Even through dungarees, the uneven terrain scraped my knees. An occasional sharp pebble, hidden from view by the scratchy green blades, pierced my tender palms.

Still I crept, determined.

The glass is all thick, cloudy bubble glass. I framed my eyes and peered inside the first window, straining hard to see.

Is this how a fly sees the world?

Aaaaand...only a utility room. Next room.

A storage room. Next.

A wolf-boy dozing in the corner. What???????

I pressed my whole face against the glass. At the other end of the room, a naked boy about my age was chained to a spike in the concrete by leg cuffs.

His brown hair was long, matted, and wild. Fur-like hair grew everywhere else, scarcely covering the red splotches and blisters.

The view: thick with flies. Was he dead?

I rapped, but the glass soaked up the sound.

136

I rapped harder.

Ow!

I sucked my knuckles until the sting subsided.

And then I raised my fist and banged, banged, banged.

He opened his eyes and saw me.

He was not dead. The flies only wanted shit and now that I could see better, there was plenty of it.

I studied him and ruminated on all the possibilities.

Gordon James was keeping him hostage.

Or someone else was, and Gordon James didn't know it, especially if the room was soundproofed.

Was the wolf-boy dangerous?

Or was he Delores' (or Gordon's) plaything?

He was fascinating to observe. He did not seem frightened or in pain, only curious about me, the way a puppy is curious about a human.

This wolf-boy was as curious about me as I was about him.

So maybe he wasn't a prisoner. Maybe he lived in the basement of the bank president's house by choice.

He didn't look gaunt. Or particularly unhealthy.

In fact, he looked like a well-fed werewolf.

But he wasn't a werewolf. And even if he lived there by choice, he shouldn't. It can't be legal, in Shelby or anywhere, to keep a human pet, even if he was a werewolf.

Which he wasn't.

But...

My heart started beating really fast.

Maybe he could be a werewolf for a little while.

Just like Gordon James could be someone else for a while.

Maybe he could be Randall Monroe McCallister St. Martin the Third, all grown up, and kept hostage by his parents.

138

Maybe he WAS Randall Monroe McCallister St. Martin the Third, all grown up, and kept hostage by his parents

Soon, I would rat on Bank President Gordon James and collect a big fat reward for turning him in.

And then I'd use the money to publicize my werewolf book and make millions of dollars. I'd be set for life.

I blew the wolf-boy a kiss (might as well, considering the role he was about to play) and crept back to the hedge.

After scoping out both sides of the sidewalk, I eased out and up, brushing the dirt and a few pieces of clinging grass from my dungarees and hands.

Then I ran all the way to Aunt Silly's, inspiration bursting through the pores of my skin.

My Werewolf Lover and Me

By Caryn Rochelle

Chapter One:
"Paw Prints"

I always feel more alive under a full moon than any place else on earth.

Even as a child, I knew, and I obeyed.

When the glowing ball in the night sky calls my name, "Carrynne! Carrynne!" I follow its summons.

Out to the night I patter.

The grass prickles my bare feet. The cool mud soothes my tender soles. The soft light is hypnotic and presses me forward to the place.

My hands reach up, up to the sky.

Then I twirl.

Round and round and round.

Electrified, I laugh and spin under that great yellow moon. My long, straight hair wraps around my naked body like a copper corkscrew.

When the moon releases me, I float home and climb back into bed, but I can never sleep. I lie there, sheet off, soaking up moonbeams and quivering.

The next day, I'm full of energy. Day by day, the energy dwindles, little by little. By the end of the month, I'm as sluggish as a winding down clock.

But then we have another full moon. The cycle repeats itself, every month.

Now that I'm nearly eighteen, the lure is stronger.

Now that I'm nearly an adult, I know why.

It's because of the paw prints.

I see them one night after I stop gyrating.

Curious, I squat to examine them.

Wolf tracks.

The moon tells me to follow them. So I do.

I glide across the top of the hill away from home and down the other side, a side I'd never seen.

As I go along, an old nursery rhyme pops into my head, and I sing it under my breath.

Wash me, and comb me,
And lay me down softly,
And lay me on a bank to dry,
That I may look pretty,
When somebody comes by.

The moon stays with me, every step. The tracks lead me to a house, open and vulnerable in a little clearing all by its forsaken self, spotlighted under the moon.

Who would build a house in the middle of an empty space and then abandon it?

The house is old and creaky. The wind bangs the loose shutters and rattles its broken glass.

My naked skin gets goosebumps, and I shiver. I wrap my arms around me, but hair and arms don't keep my skinny body very warm.

I want to go home, to pick my white nightgown off the floor where I'd dropped it, and to slide it over my head. I want to crawl between the warm covers and go right to sleep.

But I cannot resist the moon's magnetic pull.

And then I wake up.

I am in my bed at home. I am wearing my nightgown, the one I left on my floor last night when I left the house. The June sunshine warms me even through the closed curtains. What a strange dream I had!

But as I change clothes and eat cold, crunchy cereal, I think about the wolf tracks and how I managed to get home without remembering anything about the return trek. Very strange.

So after breakfast, I lock the door with my long silver key with hecatolite embedded at the end. I pocket this most precious key and head back.

Not because the moon, asleep for the day, lures me. But because I, Carrynne Amaryllis Rochester, am as curious as a bloodhound. And I am very curious about why I saw wolf tracks in my tame little neighborhood.

Maybe the wolf tracks are part of the dream, I tell myself.

I cross my backyard, hop over the little stream that runs behind our property, and lope to my hill. The hill doesn't belong to anyone, but I always call it my hill. This is where I come every month to dance and absorb the moonlight.

My feet remember the way. I soon find the wolf tracks. The imprints aren't as deep as last night, but they are still there, very real.

But is the house real, too? I have to find out.

So I follow those wolf tracks across the top of the hill and down again, across more fields. I walk for miles, many miles it seems to me, wading through scratchy thick grasses, daisies, black-eyed Susans, clover, and Queen Anne's Lace. The air smells pungent with their combined perfumes and chirrs with dark clouds of insects.

Just when I'm ready to turn back, the house emerges, looking even more pitiful in the daylight. The wolf tracks lead straight to the back yard and stop at a basement window.

So I follow the tracks and peek inside.

I see a growling beast chained to the wall; his clothes are ragged and torn. His straight brown hair hangs past his shoulders, all choppy and snarly, like he's never owned a comb. His facial hair is baby fine, scraggly and long.

I press my face against the glass for a closer look and gasp aloud.

I know the face. And when I tell you the name, you will recognize it.

This savage boy is no other than Randall Monroe McCallister St. Martin the Third.

Yes, that's right. The famous boy who went missing shortly after he was born.

I know he's the famous boy because he looks like the grown-up version of his baby picture. He has his father's eyes and his mother's mystique, even in these subhuman conditions.

Why is he here, chained inside this creepy old building where no one lives? Who did this to him?

A light clicks on inside his green eyes and grows bright, as bright as last night's moon.
He sees me. He trusts me.

And I…I…

I see him and trust him, too. The same tug I felt from the moon when it grew to its full size, I now feel from him.

Except this tug is stronger, and it tugs on my heart with a wrenching force.

I raise my hand, like I do when the moon is full. But this time, I do not raise it to the sky.

Instead, I flatten my hand on the glass, as if I can melt the glass and move through it to Randy.

Yes.

Randy.

My Randy.

My heart is already calling him Randy.

Randy follows the movement of my hand. Then he looks at me looking at him.

He holds up his right hand. A long, thick thorn is sticking out. The hand itself is red and swollen.

Help me, Carrynne.

I want to help him.

The moon brought me here to help him.

In my mind, I am already there. I am standing beside him, asking the question with my eyes.

In my mind, Randy answers with his eyes, an assent so strong the green is now phosphorescent.

In my mind, I say, "Let me help you," and I see myself lifting his hand to examine it.

But in reality, I am still standing outside the glass, and he is still on the other side, holding up the injured hand.

The yearning to help is so powerful, I feel queasy and achy. But how do I help him?

I press hard, but the thick bubble glass isn't melting under my hand. I remove my hand and look around on the ground for a big rock to break the window.

I don't see a rock. But I realize something very important.

The wolf tracks leading to the house do LEAD to the house.

But they also lead away from it.

One set of tracks point all the way to the house and stop at this window. A second set of tracks lead away from the house and toward the thick grassy field.

Both sets of tracks are wolf tracks.

Randy, I say in my mind. *You can get out?*

Of course, he replied into my mind. *And you can get in.*

I banged and banged on that glass, but I did not budge it. I saw the laugh on Randy's face, although he did not actually laugh.

Through the chink, he says.

What chink?

But Randy lowers his hand and turns away. I drop my hand; my eyes dart to and fro. I see no chink.

Desperately, I circle the house, eyes roaming over every brick and every slab of mortar.

The house is sealed up like a giant tomb. No chink anywhere.

My heart sinks like a capsized boat.

What is the size of a chink, a narrow opening, a crack?

And what is the size of me compared to it?

Even if I found the chink, I could never fit through it.

I trudge back to where the paw prints end, to the basement window, to my Randy.

The way he notices me hints he expected my return.

The way he studies me tells me he believes I will help him.

And so, with sore hand and all, he will patiently wait.

I will find a way, I tell him.

He smiles, relaxes, and lowers his hand. Yawning overtakes him, and he slumps down to the ground, stretches out, and slowly passes into sleep under my vigilance, on the other side of the window.

Bricks and bubble glass, be damned.

We are connected by our eyes and thoughts.

I think of our mystical bond for a long time.

Even though it's morning, the sky darkens. The air cools and hints of rain.

Thunder rumbles, and Randy smiles in sleep.

Then rain drips, then pitters, and then drenches me as it patters hard and fast into the ground.

It soaks the grass and plasters my clothes into my skin.

The paw prints fill with water.

I should go, I think. I should go before the paw prints disappear, and I can't find the way back.

I turn and slog to the hill. With rain pelting my eyes and running down my face, I follow my paw print map back to home, back to safety.

But at the base of the hill, before I set a single foot on its incline, an urge from way deep inside forces me to my knees.

I sink into the mud, but I don't stay on my knees.

Instead, I lie flat on the swampy ground until my face is very close to one paw print pond.

The murky water is tinged green with phosphorescence.

I inch closer and closer, until my face is hovering over the paw print, until my nose can smell the earth, and my lips can taste the dirt soup.

I begin to lap.

At first, I lap with little licks.

Then I lap with fast slurps.

I do not stop lapping until I drink the paw print dry.

JULY

July 1

Dear Maggie,

Rain.

I've been thinking a lot about rain lately. Probably because it's rained two days straight.

Thunderstorms, with all the dramatic noise and zagged light flashes, add to the scare. I mean, what would the Frankenstein movie be without the buzzing, the crackling, the dramatic weather, and then finally the shouts of, "It's alive!"

I don't know why I added rain to my first chapter. At the time, it felt like a good reason to break off the first meeting between Carrynne and Randy. And I really wanted her to drink from the werewolf's footprint, too.

But I think rain can add other moods, too. Think of the desolate sadness you feel in a gray dreary rain. Think of a storm of tears, where your face is so wet you can't tell where the tears start and the rain ends.

It's like the whole world is having a long, lonely cry. And you're outside walking in rivers of despair.

Good stuff, huh, Maggie? Now I need somewhere to put it!

July 1
Dear Maggie,

So it turns out Aunt Silly hates cooking and hardly ever cooks when I'm not here.

Wendy usually brings Dad carryout, and Aunt Silly eats whatever for dinner. That can be carryout, but carryout means stopping what she's doing to pick up the phone. She'd rather slap some bologna between two slices of bread!

I found out this morning. I had complained to Dad while he was weighing a meowing tabby. The tabby was a little scrawny for a house cat and had big, scared eyes. I had a light, but reassuring, hand on the tabby's back to hold it still.

Dad just grinned and said, "Well, Mouse, you know Prissy's doing it for you."

"Me? I didn't tell her to cook the same shit every night." I set the tabby on the table and held it in place while Dad recorded the weight. But it kept crying.

"She asked a few clients what teenagers like to eat. They told her hamburgers and hot dogs."

Dad looked up. His eyes behind his dime store glasses were twinkling.

I said, "So I can tell her to quit?"

Before I could answer, he frowned and gently moved his hands around the tabby's belly. He squinted, too. These are signs he's in deep concentration. The tabby mewed and mewed, eyes on me.

"Dad?"

"I'm afraid the tumor is back," Dad said sadly. He started stroking the cat. "And Prissy would welcome it. She never really cooked before you came."

"So what did you guys eat?"

Dad shrugged. "Carryout and whatever was in the house."

The amount of restaurants in this cutesy resort paradise is ridiculous. Carryout sounds amazing.

July 1
Dear Maggie,

Hurray! No more hot dogs and hamburgers.

I told Aunt Silly I'd rather eat carryout, and she whooped in relief. And then she brought out a folder from behind the breadbox and handed it to me. It was full of takeout flyers from every restaurant in Shelby.

"You pick," Aunt Silly said as she snuffed out her cigarette in her little ceramic ashtray on the counter. "You're in charge of dinner from now on."

She beamed at me, and I beamed at her.

July 2

Dear Maggie,

So I've been staying up super late watching old movies.

None of them are werewolf movies. All of them are mushy romance movies. And they're all fuzzy because of poor reception, no matter how fucking much I move the rabbit ears. And I keep the volume super low, so I don't wake Dad and Aunt Silly.

No, Maggie, I haven't gone soft in the head. It's part of my research. I'm trying to figure out how to write great kissing and make-out scenes.

So I sit and watch these stupid-ass movies with my notebook and pen.
It's not like I've never kissed and made out. But the boys were terrible kissers: too wet, too dry, too squeamish, too gross, and one had horrible breath, worse than a werewolf after a night of rampant killing.

None of these are right for a werewolf love story!

What's that, Maggie? What have I learned?

I've learned you can open your mouth but not use your tongue. Which is probably good for a werewolf love story, especially if the kissing happened after a hunt. Think about it, Maggie. Think about the...stuff...that might be in a werewolf's mouth after tearing people apart with his teeth!

Blech!

It's not like a werewolf carries a toothbrush and mouthwash. I'll bet nobody ever thought of that, did they? Nope!

So back to these old movies.

It seems to me what happens BEFORE the kissing is almost more important.

Like the old Greta Garbo movie I watched last night. She and John Garbin had almost four minutes (by my watch, yes, I'm timing all this) of verbal petting before launching into a wide-open (no tongue) mouth kiss.

More feelings of passion, I'm thinking, than actual passion. Longing. Gradually moving closer into each other's orbit. Maybe some panting and feeling as if the world is spinning out of control.

I know, Maggie, I know. I should write some actual sex scenes. I agree with you. I think people want to read about werewolf and human sex.

But I don't want frigid librarians and their nightcaps of magnesium cream banning my books and keeping all the copies for themselves.

If I write about sex, I can't get on the covers of <u>True Entertainment</u>, <u>Weekly Book Reviews</u>, and <u>Teens Today magazines</u>. And you know my book is destined for this.

So, Maggie, I need sexy kissing scenes. They must be light on the necking and the petting but sexy enough to make readers squirm...A LOT.

July 3

Dear Maggie,

So when I say Aunt Silly sells her jewelry everywhere, I mean everywhere.

Yesterday afternoon, we actually went into a place called, get this original name, Pelican Bar.

It really ought to be called Surf Your Turf.

It's the place where all the tourist men ditch their tourist wives for a while.

It's not the first time we went into this bar. But it's the first time I'm telling you about Lionel.

Lionel looks like he used to be really hot. But now he looks like charred meat that people forgot to take off the grill because they were too drunk. You know, when you get back up in the morning and stagger over to the grill and there it is, a wizened lump, all that's left of a twenty-two dollar cut.

That's Lionel.

Anyway, he sits there every day, looking like he's about to cry and hoping that his wife has left enough on his bank card that he can pick up someone else's wife and bring her back before either spouse finds out.

But what if...
What if, Maggie, he forgets to pick someone up?

What if he just sits there drinking and moping that he can't get anyone because his card is maxed out?

What if he sits there until the sun — and his pecker — goes down and the moon goes up?

And then what if a very sexy hairy woman walks into the bar and sits right down beside him?

Good stuff, right? Here's how I developed the rest of it. I just have to figure out how to word the beginning.

And change Lionel's name to something else, of course. Because, well, you know, Maggie.

Lionel, of course, does a double take. He's never seen a woman so hairy. And so beautiful. And then he remembered his friend Joe, before he passed, had set up a blind date.

For him. For tonight.

And she smiles at him. With blood on her teeth and human flesh on her lips, she smiles at him.

And Lionel, uncertain what to think, bangs the side of his head a couple of times, glances down at his near empty drink, and then thinks, "Oh, what the heck."

Lionel turns back to her and smiles. "Drink?"

The hairy sexy lady shakes her head. She places her paw on his thigh and nods her head to the door.

Lionel leaves his drink and follows her out the door.

All you can hear that night are loud howls. The loudest howls anyone ever heard from a human or werewolf.

The next day, Lionel is back at the bar. His clothes are torn; his face is scratched; and one eye is swollen shut.

But he is grinning.

July 3

Dear Maggie,

Would you believe even the meat shoppe buys Aunt Silly's jewelry? It's true!

A place that grinds up animals into human food wants to sell chatoyant gems on delicate wire.

Personally, I can think of some humans who would make great food for animals. But that's for the werewolves to sort out.

We also left quite a few jewelry pieces at a soup and sandwich shoppe. This shoppe also sells locally grown dried herbs and locally crafted useless trinkets.

Both places took a lot of her jewelry. And both places gave her fat wads of cash for the jewelry she's already sold.

I didn't bring home any meat, soup, sandwiches, herbs, or trinkets. But the shoppe did sell these little parchments posters that featured delicately drawn herbs and little verses in quaint script.

One caught my eye, and I bought it.

Here's what it says in my best imitation of the writing:

Take chamomile to beguile

And sleep, sleep, sleep.

Take Rosa Damascena

Grow wiser than Athena

And sleep, sleep, sleep

Take lavender, you scavenger

And sleep, sleep, sleep

Take valerian, my canine heroine

And sleep, sleep, sleep

Take lemon balm, heal his palm

And sleep, sleep, sleep

Take passion flower, and within the hour

You'll sleep, sleep, sleep

I didn't get a chance to sneak over to Gordon James' house today. But I will as soon as I can!

July 4
Dear Maggie,

Fourth of July in Shelby is NOT the same as Fourth of July in North Lyons. I hate gatherings of people, and I hate the way all the fireworks terrify the animals. Aunt Silly likes people, so she spent the day doing social shit downtown.

Dad and I hung out at his office and took care of all the luxury pets the selfish tourists boarded for the night, so they could have their fun instead of shielding their poor little scared animals from Armageddon.

In the middle of the commotion, a sudden thought came to me. Each boom was probably like the last sound a werewolf must hear when someone fires a silver bullet through his heart.

Would Randy know this sound? Would Carrynne?

And all of a sudden, Maggie, I became afraid.

I became afraid that their love might get torn apart by Randy's father or the mad scientist or maybe even a lynch mob. I had not thought about these possibilities until now. I mean, Randy is a werewolf. And his father and a mad scientist ARE controlling him.

So WHAT IF someone with a gun...

And I resolved in that moment to NOT let that happen.

My world's greatest werewolf love story MUST have a happy ending.

Maggie, it was all I could do to keep from sobbing out loud!

July 5
Dear Maggie,

As I'm heading over to Dad's office today, I almost stepped on a poor yipping bluish brown Yorkie.

Fucking tourists!

They plop their dogs into their giant handbags and off they go!

The dogs, of course, are panting with excitement. They also bark at everyone they pass. So the sidewalks during prime shopping hours (ten in the morning until two in the afternoon) sound louder than Dad's office during an epidemic of kennel cough!

Seriously, Maggie, at least twice a week I'm bringing a lost dog to Dad's until its stupid owner realizes she dropped it.

To settle the Yorkie down as I carried it down the sidewalk, I sing. Like I said, I've done this so much, I have my own lost dog theme song.

"Oh, where, oh, where
"Has my little dog gone?
"Oh, where, oh, where
"Can he be?
"With his ears cut short
"And his tail cut long,
"Oh, where, oh, where

"Can he be?"

The dog had just finished his lunch (on the house, I might add) when the owner showed up, some skinny bitch with sprayed hair and sparkly glasses on a chain around her neck.

She just picked up her Yorkie, sneered at Wendy, and strolled out the door while nuzzling her dog without so much as a thank you!

July 5
Dear Maggie,

Tonight after I showered, I stood at the window in my white nightgown and gazed out into the darkness, thinking about the hairy boy in Gordan James' basement and fingering Aunt Silly's moonstone necklace.

If he was a real werewolf, I'd will my thoughts across the yard and through the night, straight to his mind. We would be so close, we could think each other's thoughts even through the distance.

I closed my eyes and stretched out my fingers, trying to feel Carrynne's yearning for Randy. I felt the tugs of her heart for him within my own heart. I pictured her lost and sad and wet in the rain, seeking the other half of her soul that is beyond her reach.

I tasted the salt of my tears.

I opened my eyes and looked longingly at my typewriter. I was not Carrynne, and "it" was not a werewolf.

But I was Caryn's God and only I could make Carrrynne and her werewolf come alive and find each other.
Dad and Aunt Silly were old and needed their sleep. Typing was out of the question.

But...I couldn't lose this moment!

So I tiptoed into the living room to Aunt Silly's desk, opened a drawer, and grabbed a fresh yellow pad and pencil.

Then I closed the drawer ALL THE WAY and tiptoed back to bed.

I woke up at some point with my face on the pad. It was wet where I had drooled on it. I was still clutching the pencil. I grinned to myself, slid my magical tools beneath my pillow and switched off the light.

This morning, I typed it all out while eating breakfast.

Pretty good, huh?

Chapter 2:
"The Walking Stick"

When I awake the next morning, my skin is damp, and my bed is sopping.

My clothes lay in a puddled pile. Wet footprints streak the wooden floor.

My knee throbs like the drum of a marching band. I vaguely recall twisting it in the slick grass while skipping home in the rainstorm.

I remember sitting on the kitchen floor icing the knee with cubes from the freezer.

I remember pacing the floor by night, restless and hungry.

I remember the moon's call…
And now, here I am.

I'm lying in my bed, in pain, in the gray morning.

The outside is overcast and drizzly. It sends a damp chill to my bones.

My knee is tender and oversized. If I'm going to see Randy, I will need my father's cane.

I get dressed and eat cereal. Then I go to my parents' closet, pushing back the clothes and holding my breath against the moth balls, to his old cane.

But it's also a special cane. It is made of rowan wood. My grandfather, a healer, walked with it. My father, also a healer, walked with it.

Now I must walk with it, if I want to heal Randy. It's a beautiful golden brown cane, very knobby, with natural circles up and down its staff.

It's the perfect walking stick for a walk over a hill and to my Randy. I hobble around the house with it, for practice.

Then I leave the house, pocket the key, and limp over marshy ground to the hill.

It's a long, long, long, long, long slippery trudge to the top.

When I get there, I look for the paw prints, all over the wide hill, but they're gone. Either the rain washed them away, or the mud filled them in, or both.

Maybe whoever imprisoned Randy erased them.

The only marks on the ground are the imprints of my rowan cane and my muddy sneakers.

I raise my hand and shake my fist! I will not be stopped!
I cock my head and listen for Randy's voice in my mind, for direction.

But I hear only my own muttering thoughts.

It's this way, I tell myself, my wet soles going squish-squish-squish as I head for the farthest side of the hill. It must be this way.

When I reach the edge, I carefully inch down the steep treacherous side, digging in my heels and the tip of my rowan cane so I don't slip and roll to my death.

This does nothing for my throbbing knee. And it takes forever.

But I finally reach the bottom. The grassy field is now rivulets of water. The wildflowers hang limp with yesterday's rain; the muggy air smells of rain and mud.

The paw prints, my map, are gone.

I waver and then straighten my shoulders with confidence in our bond, mine and Randy's.

Since I cannot walk with a guide, I will walk by instinct.

I turn around to study the hill and burn its location in my memory.

I turn back to study the endless swamp.

I close my eyes and begin to walk. As I walk through the sloshing field, I sing the nursery rhyme I sang the first time:

.

"Wash me, and comb me,
"And lay me down softly,
"And lay me on a bank to dry,
"That I may look pretty,
"When somebody comes by."

But after singing it a few times, I stop. The song doesn't FEEL right.

I open my eyes and turn around again. The hill is still in sight, but now it's only a tiny speck of a hill.

A shudder of fear runs through me, a fear of losing the hill, losing my way to Randy, and losing my way back.

I tremble at the thought of wandering through the open field, eternally lost.

As I'm thinking, I realize I'm sinking.

I sink past my ankles, and my heart sinks lower than that.

Where is my Randy, I say in my soul. Where is the old, lonely house holding my hairy beast boy?

I'm up to my knees now, and I don't care. I'm crying like rain, stuck in leftover rain, and clinging to the only stick that can keep me safe.

I cry harder; I arch my head and howl. My howls are screaming howls, howls of despair, howls of longing, for the Randy I need to help.

If you're in the middle of an empty field crying up a storm, does anyone hear? Does anyone care?

I care!

And I sing, "Oh, where, oh where, has my Randy boy gone? Oh where, or where can he be? With his hair messed up and his paw all thorned? Oh where, or where has he gone?"

And I sing louder and harder. "Oh, where, oh where, has my Randy boy gone? Oh where, or where can he be? With his hair all messed up and his paw all thorned? Oh where, or where has he gone?"

"Oh, where, oh where, has my Randy boy gone? Oh where, or where can he be? With his hair all messed up and his paw all thorned? Oh where, or where has he gone?"

"Oh, where, oh where, has my Randy boy

gone? Oh where, or where can he be? With his hair all messed up and his paw all thorned? Oh where, or where has he gone?"

"Oh, where, oh where, has my Randy boy gone? Oh where, or where can he be? With his hair all messed up and his paw all thorned? Oh where, or where has he gone?"

I sing until I'm hoarse. I'm now up to my waist and in danger of drowning. I slap my face to shut me up. My wails turn to snuffling and the occasional low moan.

I make myself turn back. I drag my cane with ferocious strength through the thick glop and wade through the stream to the speck of the growing hill.

The climb up takes hours. The climb down takes more.

Or so it seems.

The trudge home has no start or stop. It seems as if I've always trudged, wet and dirty and cold.

At home, I strip my muddy garments and sit naked, legs splayed, on the kitchen floor tile, icing my angry knee.

The rowan cane, my protector against the fallout of storms, rests beside me, guarding my key. My knee does not let me move the rest of the day.

If I try, it objects with searing pain, and I yelp, which makes my scratchy throat burn like fire.

So I sit all day on the kitchen floor in the humid house and let the ice and my damp skin cool all of me except my brain, which is feverish for Randy.

I shiver and shake.

By evening, the ice is warm runny water; I'm starving and have to pee. So I go to the bathroom to pee. Then I put dry clothes on and figure out dinner.

I rummage in the refrigerator and find a package of hamburger, which I cook very rare, nibbling bites of the raw ground meet as I shape the patties; it cools my scalding throat.

My parents like hamburgers. When I was a child, we ate them a couple times a week.

Hamburgers are a good choice.

I also heat oil, slice potatoes, and fry them; I toss a lettuce and tomato salad.

With each activity, times passes. The day falls away; the night creeps up.

Soon, I know, the moon will invoke me.

Tonight, I know, I must not obey the call, for the sake of my knee.

And for the sake of Randy, whom I'll never help if I keep walking on my sore knee.

Besides, the ground is soaking wet. Any paw prints made on that hill will vanish into the earth.

Tonight, I stay home. Soon, it's time for bed.

As I lie in bed, desire for Randy runs through me like an untamed beast and makes everything pound like my knee until the pounding erupts through me in growls and snarls.

But father's cane lies on the floor against the door. And the key is safely tucked underneath my pillow.

Drowsiness overtakes me; breathlessness relaxes into easy breaths.

The full moon does not call me.

I sleep soundly, all through the night.

The rowan cane is a good cane.

July 6
Dear Maggie,

One of the bakeries that takes Aunt Silly's jewelry always sets out a plate of free desserts. The desserts are different each day, probably shit they couldn't sell the previous day.

So far this summer I've tried layered chiffon cake drizzled with chocolate, wedges of rhubarb pie and banana cream pie, cubes of colored gelatin, ice cream snowballs with strawberry sauce, pudding topped with maraschino cherries, pineapple upside down cake, squares of carrot cake with cream cheese frosting, and lots of cookies: peanut butter, sugar, shortbread, oatmeal, and fruit bars.

Dad really likes the coffee from this bakery, too. I think I'll bring him one...and one for Wendy, too.

July 6
Dear Maggie

I was rereading parts of my werewolf story, the parts about hamburger. Even though Aunt Silly has given up on hamburgers, hamburger meat was now part of the plot. If I get rid of it now, I'll have to change too much.

And if I change too much, I won't finish before my eighteenth birthday. It's better to leave it alone. Don't you agree, Maggie?

I mean, it's not like my werewolf story is about real life!

July 7
Dear Maggie,

I finally had the chance to sneak back to "you know where" today.

"Heading out to see Dad," I called to Aunt Silly once she was busy on a phone call.

She waved her hand at me, the one holding her cigarette, and I slinked out the door.

I did pop into the office to say, "Hi" to Wendy...and to check out "the lay of the land."

"He's in surgery," Wendy said apologetically as she answered the ringing phone.

It was really sad, too...broken leg on a schnauzer whose stupid owner didn't deserve anything living, not even a houseplant.

But I had my alibi.

I sauntered aimlessly down the street except my sauntering wasn't aimless. I was heading for Fifth Street, 666 Fifth Street, to be exact.

I slowed my pace slightly as I neared the tall boxy house with the old, gnarled rowan trees. I scanned my surroundings from the corners of my eyes.

Then I dropped and scrambled between the tall, thick hedges. I crawled as quickly as I could over the lumpy yard that ground pain into my knees and palms with every forward movement.

I felt the dull ache of pebbles, long embedded into the hardpacked dirt; I felt the sharp pricks of pointed grass and stray twigs. But nothing swayed me from "his" window. When I reached it, I peered inside.

"Randy" was still there, still chained to a spike in the concrete by leg cuffs. He's still hairy and dirty, and he's still naked (Maggie, you should see the size of his...well, you should see it) and he's still covered with red splotches and blisters. The floor is still covered in shit and flies.

I raised my hand, covered with powdered dirt and grass stains. And then I soundlessly banged on that bubble glass.

He opened his eyes. They darted around until they rested on me. He cocked his head a little, like a puzzled German shepherd puppy.

Did he remember me from last time? Was that recognition in his eyes?

Was it?

Maggie, I don't know how long he stared at me while I stared at him. But

178

when I came...to...I...the story was so...vibrant...and alive...in my mind.

I ran all the way home and wrote until bedtime. Aunt Silly was so understanding, she brought my hamburger dinner to me.

Yes, hamburgers. I guess we can't eat carryout every night.

But I was so into my werewolf story, Aunt Silly could have served up mulch, and I would have dove into it.

"The potatoes are a little crunchy," she apologized.

I stopped typing to try one. She was right.

"They're too thick," I told her. "You have to slice them really thin."

Aunt Silly grinned. "I'll try harder. I can't serve shitty food to a famous novelist."

Suddenly, fresh inspiration hit me like a thunderbolt.

I'm going to make Aunt Silly a character in my novel. Won't she be surprised?

July 8

Dear Maggie,

I spent most of the day at Dad's office, cleaning cages, restocking supplies, and filing for Wendy.

Dad had a lot of appointments, a few dogs that needed stitches, one cat that kept throwing up, and a house call.
But while I worked, I came up with ideas for making Aunt Silly a character in my book.

I can't wait to get home!!!

July 8

Dear Maggie,

I have another chapter done, hurray!!!
And I'm out of ideas, boo!!!

Writing the world's greatest werewolf story before my eighteenth birthday is NOT going to happen if most of my ideas come from Gordan James' backyard.

Between you and me, Maggie, it's hard finding the time to sneak over there. I'm surprised the bank president hasn't caught me snooping around. And I'm surprised Dad and Aunt Silly haven't noticed how long it takes me to get back and forth from the house to the office and from the office to the house.

I'm counting on them being so busy they never notice.

Can I get as lucky with Gordan James?

Anyway, here is chapter three...with Aunt Silly playing a role in the story.

I think it turned out fucking amazing. And I hope she likes it!!!

Chapter 3:
"Not a Regular Drink of Water"

The next morning my knee is better, and I make up my mind. I will go to town and see Rosie.
Some people think Rosie is crazy, but I am not one of them.
So after I eat breakfast, I wrap the last of the raw hamburger in plenty of wax paper to contain the scent and tuck it into my beaded purse.
Then I lay the rowan cane near the door before I lock it and pocket the key. That was not as easy as it

sounds. The rowan cane was not in front of my door when I woke up. I had to look all over the house for it. When I couldn't find it, I looked all over the yard for it. Finally I found it, under the wild roses, speckled with fresh blood.

"Silly cane," I say to it as I smear the blood on the grass. "What an adventure you had last night!"

I walk down the drive toward the long sidewalk to the corkscrew road that leads me to town, wondering how the cane left by itself and where it had decided to go.

I pass adorable little A-framed shoppes with colorful cloth awnings and wooden signs hanging from wrought iron. There's a soap shoppe and a candle shoppe and a clock shoppe, and what looks like a head shoppe and jewelry shoppe and dippy clothes shoppes, you get the idea.

Finally, I come to Rosie's place. The tape is coming loose from her cardboard sign: Free Fortunetelling.

I am not fooled. Nothing is free. Not even Rosie. Her clients always pay.

I push open the rusty metal door. A bell jingles. I sneeze against the dust. Rosie is standing in the middle of the dark room, stirring a cauldron.

Rosie wears these tent-like dresses in bright prints, like orange and green or yellow and magenta. She wears clay jewelry she makes herself: long beaded necklaces and dangly earrings off gold wires: hoops, bells, zebras, trout, spires, rutabagas. You name it, she probably has earrings that look like it. She wears a bandana over her blonde, curly hair.

"Whatcha makin' today, Rose?" I ask, peering inside.

"Soup," Rosie grins.

I chuckle. She's always making soup.

I remove the package from my purse. "I brought hamburger."

Rosie cackles happily. She dumps the ground meat into the pot and stirs. A noxious smell rises from the thick oily liquid, just how she likes it.

"How can Rosie help today?"

"I need a map."

"To where?"

I tell Rosie my story while she uncaps smudged bottles and tosses green flakes into her soup. At the last pinch, I swear I hear a scream from the bottle of the pot. But maybe I am only hearing my own desperation.

When I finish talking. Rosie nods and sets the ladle down. She hobbles to another room and returns holding a silver chain. A single moonstone dangles from it.

The moonstone is round and bluish white, with splashes of gray, black, pink, and cobalt.

"Take this and wear it," Rose said. "It knows the way to your soul mate."

I clasp the chain around my neck and thank Rosie.

"And take this."

Rosie hands me a piece of dirty linen tied with a frayed gray ribbon that used to be white, I can tell. I sniff the sachet and wrinkle my nose at the pungent smell.

"Healing herbs," Rosie explains.

I start for the door.

"Wait," she said. "Have some soup for the journey."

I wrinkle my nose. "It smells bad."

She shrugs. "It's your hamburger."

I smile. "Not anymore. And I had a big breakfast."

I take another way to the hill, cross the top to the other side, and down. I slog for miles though the flooded fields, thick grasses, daisies, black-eyed Susans, and Queen Anne's Lace. They plaster themselves to my skin and capris, as if to hold me back.

But I have a moonstone around my neck, a beast boy in my heart, and a bold purpose in my soul. Nothing can stop me.

I walk for days, it seems. Once or twice, or more, I stop to check the necklace. It's still glowing blue-ish white, so I am going the right way.

I keep trudging, famished. I am not sorry I turned down the foul-smelling soup with mysterious seasonings from no-label bottles. At least with hamburger, I know what I'm eating.

The house emerges, looking less pitiful than I recalled it, but maybe I'm used to seeing it, and its shoddy exterior no longer catches me by surprise.

I see no wolf tracks this time, but the full moon has gone away for the month. I let the moonstone lead me to the basement window.

Randy is chained to the wall, and his raggedy clothes are nearly threadbare. His straight brown hair still hangs past his shoulders, all choppy and snarly, and his facial hair is still baby fine, scraggly, and even longer than last time.

He's not sleeping. He's sitting on his haunches, as if he's expecting me. But it's his injured hand that breaks my heart. It's swollen to ten times it's natural size, all red and dripping thick yellow goo.

I waited for you, Carrynne. I waited, and you did not come.

Oh, Randy!

I cry and cry and cry at the sight of him, imprisoned, infected, and in pain.

Who did this to you, Randy? Who is hurting you?

My father.

Your father! Why would your father hurt you?

I am heir to the great St. Martin fortune. But my father has another purpose for me.

I will help you! See? I brought medicine!

Do you know what I am, Carrynne?

Yes. You are my soul mate.

What else am I, Carrynne?

You are a werewolf!

He relaxes at my words, and I rejoice. He trusts me as I trust him. Now he can confide in me. And then we can make a plan to help him.

How so I get the medicine to you, Randy? I cannot get in the crack, and you cannot get out until the full moon.

Set the medicine under the window. It knows the way in.

I set the sachet on the ground, but it does not move. I nudge it with my sneaker.

"Go medicine," I say aloud to encourage it. "Go to Randy and heal his paw."

Randy laughs aloud. The medicine doesn't move.

It will, Carrynne. Don't worry. Do you want to hear about my mother?

Yes, Randy.

He stretches out on the concrete and clasps his hands behind his neck. He looked very comfortable on the cold, hard floor, my silly Randy.

My mother is a descendent from the famous Beast of Gévaudan. Do you know about the beast, Carrynne?

Of course, I know all about the Beast of Gévaudan. It's a famous werewolf.

My father married her, thinking he could use her to take over the world. But when she learned of his evil plan, she tried to escape, and he killed her with a silver bullet. I cried over her bloodied and matted hide for a very long time.

I feel my heart tear to shreds for the baby wolf boy who lost his mother, and I start to cry.

And then, Carrynne, he had me.
Oh, Randy, what do you mean?

In my vulnerability, he lassoed me, dragged me to the cellar, and locked me up. He kept me here until I was old enough.

Old enough for what?

For breeding.

I clench my fists.

Randy, why don't you overpower him when he brings you food?

Because he never brings me food. I must catch and kill my own food.

But you're locked up!

During the full moon, my soul seeps through the crack, and I run free. I catch and kill enough food to last the entire month.

This is when I notice the carcass bits across the basement floor like pieces of leftover steak and the dark splotches over the concrete.

Like you ran free last month, Randy?

Yes, Carrynne.

I drank out of your paw print, Randy.

I know, Carrynne. I hoped you would.

I want to run free with you, Randy! Take me next time!

No, Carrynne. It's not safe?

Why not?

I always run out of food before the end of the month, Carrynne. And I grow very hungry, desperately hungry. I might mistake you for food.

I'll bring you food. I'll bring you food and leave it outside when the moon is full. Then you can eat the food, and you will not harm me, and I can run free with you, Randy.

I love you, Carrynne.

I love you, Randy!

I start to cry. I feel sad and lonely on the other side of the wall.

Can't you try to escape? Werewolves are very strong!

My father has an evil scientist helping him. The scientist is beating me with a stick made out of mountain ash and immobilizing me with aconite. My father is not smart enough to do it himself. I can get as far as the hill for food but no further.

Aconite! This is terrible!

I know all about mountain ash. It is a mystical tree that repels werewolves.

I also know all about aconite. The plant has teeny white eyes staring out from bluish purple petals that look like the hoods on the cloaks of medieval monks. Their stalks are a sickly yellow-green.

And it poisons werewolves.

Knowing that someone was controlling my Randy with it makes me very, very, very angry.

Yes. If you can help me find the scientist and where he keeps the aconite, I will be able to escape. I will be able to run past the hill. You won't have to come to me. I will come for you. And then we can run free together forever.

July 8

Dear Maggie,

It's funny how a summer night can be exciting and serene at the same time. When I sit outside on the porch with Dad and Aunt Silly, all of us hardly talking, you'd think we'd enjoy the silence.

But actually the insects are so loud, we have to shout to make ourselves heard. The lightning bugs fill the yard with their little electric lights, like tiny aliens in a search party.

Dad just puffs on his pipe. Aunt Silly rocks in her mother's old rocker. I sit on an old ottoman and hug my knees, soaking up impressions.

Aunt Silly told me once that Dad revels in the quiet company. I would, too, if I listened to frantic barking and bitchy people all day. It can get pretty loud in Dad's office. And I ain't talking about the animals!

This is how Aunt Silly explained it to me one day: "Your dad's always been that way. He's not one for yackety yak. He enjoys some company, but he doesn't want to mentally process it, especially after dealing with jabbering clients all day."

So Aunt Silly and I understand why Dad needs this time. So we give it to him.

I love my dad.

July 9

Dear Maggie,

Aunt Silly was spending most of the day making jewelry, so I spent most of the day at Dad's office doing miscellaneous office stuff.

He had one appointment after the next with no break, not even to take a piss. Fucking tourists!

They feed their pets candy, take them off leashes and let them get trampled, and drag them into all the boutiques in the heat and humidity, all the while they're slurping on their iced drinks and forgetting their fluffy toys need water.

Then they bring their poor dehydrated little balls of fur to Dad for IVs!!!!

So I went to the Golden Egg Café brought back two orders of Monte Cristos and waffle fries for Dad and me. And I brought him coffee, black coffee, the way he likes it.

OK, I did have to use Dad's bank card to pay for it.

On the way there and back, I tried to devise a scheme to get me back to Gordon James' yard and his wolf boy "house guest."

Both times, I had to pass The Clock Shoppe. Both times, I looked away.

And then I remembered.

I had wanted to use my nightmares of The Clock Shoppe and The Clock Man in my werewolf story.

What if I made that the focus of chapter four?

What if Carrynne, who is missing her Randy so much, goes off in search of a magic clock that "adjusts" time so she can spend more time with Randy?

A month is too long to wait for another full moon, I mused, but so is sixty seconds when you're apart from your wolf mate.

Maggie, I was so full of ideas when I got back to Dad's office, that I almost forgot why I left.

"Mouse, what's this?" Dad said as he walked a client and her Siamese cat toward the door.

I held up the bag and cup. "I brought dinner."

Dad smiled, a weary smile. "Let me wash up. We can eat in my office."

Maggie, you should have seen how fast I found pen and paper to jot down all my ideas before I forgot them!

July 10
Dear Maggie,

Aunt Silly spent the day making jewelry again. Wendy was back in the office, so Dad told me to stay home and work on the werewolf story.

He told me the good news over breakfast. Before he left the table, he brushed my hand and said, "I knew you'd write it, Mouse. I believe in you."

Maggie, I can't let him down!

So Aunt Silly spent the day at the kitchen table make jewelry. Dad spent all day healing the animals of Shelby.

And I spent all day clacking out chapter four. I must confess, Maggie, this was the hardest chapter I've written so far. It was like living in your worst nightmare for a full day. At one point, my blood felt so cold, my teeth were chattering, and the hairs on my arms stood straight up.

Boy, was I glad the bedroom door won't shut!

While I wrote, the normal everyday sounds floated in and kept me from hysteria. I listened to the faint sounds of pop melodies, the drone of quarterly news reports, and silence from the radio when the phone rang, and Aunt Silly turned the dial down to talk to a customer.

Sometimes she would get distracted by the conversation and forget to turn the radio back up after she hung up. When the quiet house became bone chillingly silent, I'd call out, "Aunt Silly!"

"Whaddya need, Caryn?" she'd yell.

"I need music!"

Then with Three Phils and Mr. Mash, The Pony Players, Joan Reedsy, and Jammin' Tucker's Who's Who Band jamming their hit songs, I managed to transfer my horrifying impressions of my longest-lasting terror from inside my mind onto the paper.

Chapter 4:
"The Clock Man"

A month is too long to wait for another full moon, but so is sixty seconds when you're apart from your wolf mate.

But the world is full of people who can bend the laws of nature, and many of them live near me.

Rosie is one. The Clock Man is another.

The Clock Man keeps his shoppe on the same street as Rosie's shoppe. After leaving Randy's house, I head there.

But this walk is full of twists and turns; it is not a straight walk. But the moonstone glow an intense blueish white, so I know the way is true.

It is dark when I arrive. The sign hanging on the dented metal door is turned to "closed." I hiss and bang, but the door stays locked.

So I turn my feet toward home to wait for tomorrow.

At home, I am out of hamburger, but I am not out of other food. I make dinner and howl at the moon while I eat, giggling to myself between howls.

I will make a fine mate for a werewolf, I think.

I go to bed early with the key underneath my pillow and the rowan cane at my door so tomorrow will come quickly.

The next day, I head out early, but not too early, so I'm not waiting outside for The Clock Man to open his shoppe. Before I leave, I lay the rowan cane near the door before I lock up.

That's not as easy as it sounds because the rowan cane had, again, left its post at my bedroom door. After a long search, I found the cane down the window well and nearly covered with gravel.

This time the blood is dry, so I rinse it with the garden hose and then wipe it clean on the grass. I talk to the cane all the way back to the house.

"You are more than a silly cane," I tell it. "You are a naughty cane. If you won't stay by my door, I will chain you there."

I give the cane a little smack and then set it into place. Then I pocket the key and hurry. The way is not far, only a little past Rosie's, and soon I am standing outside the dented metal door once again.

Unlike many shoppes, this door has no jingling bell to welcome me inside. It's dark and cold and filled with the disjointed cacophony of thousands of ticking clocks.

No one has ever seen The Clock Man. Customers just take the clocks they want to buy, leave their money on the counter, and go back out the door.

It's impossible to steal from The Clock Man. If someone tries, the door locks all by itself and will not unlock until the money is there.

So if no one has ever seen The Clock Man, how do I know he is real?

Because everyone says so.

Because the best clocks in the whole world are found here. The clock chooses the customer as much as the customer chooses it. Clocks made by The Clock Man are beautiful to behold. They never break, and they always keep perfect time.

Once someone buys a clock from The Clock Man, they never buy another clock from anyone else.

Today, I am here to buy a clock. But I don't want a clock that keeps perfect time. I want a clock that will make all time disappear, except the time I want, the time with Randy. No other time is important to me.

Walls are jammed with clocks.
The cabinets and shelves are full of
clocks. Tables are crowded with
clocks; I step over clocks on the
floor.

Clear clocks, wooden clocks,
grandfather clocks, cuckoo clocks,
alarm clocks, kitchen wall clocks,
golden clocks, clocks that tick,
silent clocks, wristwatches, and
clocks with heavy pendulums.

They tick and tock out of time
with each other, a caterwauling of
deafening sounds: tick, tack, tick,
tack; ttok-ttak, ttok-ttak;
kochikochi, kachikochi; chiku taku,
tick-tock; tick-tock; tika, taka,
tika, taka.

Hundreds of clock faces watch me
inch around the room; they point
accusing clock hands at me, the
stranger in their realm. I'm very
conscious of my lack of gears and
metallics, of flesh which is soft and
easily pierced and the fact I've edged
myself in a far corner of the room,
covered only by a sheet.

Suddenly, the sheet whips aside,
and a bloated face is staring down at
me.

His face is round and pale like
the Man in the Moon but without all
its shadows. His hair is blond-gray
and sparsely covers his scalp.

His eyes are more gray than
blue. But the color was less important
than what he says:

"A mind not to be changed by place or
time.
The mind is its own place, and in
itself
Can make a heav'n of hell, a hell of
heav'n."

I tell him, "I don't wish to alter time. I just want to skip any time that's not important to me."

He yanks the sheet back, hiding himself from me.

I yank it open.

He's gone.

But before me is a short passageway that leads to a dark room.

I cross the line and walk across the creaking boards.

In the center of that room is one square wooden table. In the middle of the table is a clock. It's made of brass and has an oval face with a green phosphorescent iris in the middle. It's pupil is a black hole. From the depths of the black hole, I sense, although I cannot see, a tiny little phosphorescent light.

I feel the clock looking at me like I'm looking at it. And I can almost hear it think: *I am the time you want all the time you want the time you want I am the time you want all the time you want the time you want I am the time you want all the time you want the time you want.*

I feel dizzy and debate if I want to take it home.

It debates the same thing.

Finally, we reach a mutual understanding.

I lift it off the table, and I think I hear it sigh. It's heavier than it looks, and I struggle to lug it to the front of the store.

This room seems almost bright and sunny compared to the cramped rear room that no longer has a clock on its only table.

I set the clock on the floor and take my little paisley coin purse out of my back pocket. I untwist it and dump the money on the counter.

Then I pick up my clock and march to the door.

The door opens by itself.

Joyful and triumphant, I carry my clock out into moonlight and all the way home.

July 11

Dear Maggie.

Just a quick note because I have to pack.

Aunt Silly and I are leaving on a short road trip.

We're driving into ANOTHER village for a couple days. It's not far, just an hour away. Aunt Silly has a few clients there, enough that she goes out three or four times a year. So I guess she owns a car and drives, after all.

The point, Maggie, is that it's a day trip, not a European tour.

And it was Dad who suggested we stay. Yippee (written with great sarcasm).

That happened last night while we were sitting on the back porch not talking while Dad smoked his pipe and fireflies dotted the yard with fairy light flashes.

"Prissy, who don't you and Caryn stay a few days?" Dad said after Aunt Silly shared her plans.

Even in the dark, I could see Aunt Silly grin. "Fred, I was going to say the exact thing!"

I scowled. But before I could retort, Dad smiled and winked at me.

"I know what you're thinking, Mouse," he said.

"You're sure? Because I think you're going to 'reassure me' that this village is not typically a boring-ass tourist village. Except now. Because it's summer."

Dad removed his pipe. "You're off the scent. Munsonville is actually a year-round attraction for tourists, but only if they like to fish. It's not a commercial attraction the way Shelby is. In fact, all life there moves at a slug's pace. The village's entire industry depends on it."

"Who the fuck cares? And don't tell me that a bunch of fucking fishermen care about Aunt Silly's jewelry."

"Caryn Alaina," Dad said.

Dad hardly ever uses my real names, and he especially doesn't use them together. When this happens, I know he is losing patience with me.

"What?" I asked, playing stupid.

"I think you will find plenty of inspiration for your story." He knocked the ashes into the tray and stretched. "Prissy, I'm taking a shower and turning in."

After he went inside, I asked Aunt Silly to explain what Dad meant about "finding inspiration" there. But she was just as short with me. She mumbled something about being tired and that we'd talk on the road.

This morning she's insisting I bring a notebook and some pens. Maybe two notebooks.

So back to packing.

And then off we go...

July 12
Dear Maggie,

Traveling with Aunt Silly is a lot different than traveling with Dad.

First of all, she doesn't drive a brand-new Ferdinand XGE with air conditioning. No, she drives an old Mode 9. It's full of rust and dents, but it powers up like a beast and has a super smooth ride.

Plus, we both smoked our lungs out all the way there. None of the Modes, even the new ones, have air conditioning. So we had to keep the windows down. Otherwise, we would have melted like fat in a frying pan!

So as I said, Aunt Silly is lots of fun most of the time. And she was even more fun on the road because she wasn't thinking about work or humping to keep up with orders.

We could just joke and smoke and crank up the radio as far it went...which wasn't very far! The radio is old and crackly. Plus with the windows down, you could hardly hear what song was playing.

During the first half, we luxuriated in our new-found freedom. I stared at the open fields. Some had golden wheat, and some had giant yellow sunflowers. I smoked and bopped to the music.

After half an hour we came to a town, and she slowed the Mode. It's called Jenson, and its mostly a college town, Aunt Silly said. The main strip is called, get this, His Majesty's Row. This strip has a bunch of towering old Gothic houses where all the rich fucks of long ago used to live.

Now many of those old homes are part of the campus. The main college building looked ancient. It had six stories and turrets and a sign on the lawn: "Jenson College of the Liberal Arts."

"This is a nice school," Aunt Silly hinted.

I glared at her. "Fuck off."

I was tired of this conversation, from her, from everyone. World famous rich authors don't need fucking college. Dad stopped bringing up "college" two years ago. So I sure as fuck didn't need to hear it from her.

But even after we drove out of Jenson and past more fields, Aunt Silly stayed quiet, and I stayed sullen. We were having so much fun until she became a bitch. But I missed the fun we were having until she turned on me, so I decided to be the adult.

"Why is Munsonville a good place to write my werewolf novel?" I asked.

"It has a haunted house."

"Big deal."

I thought she'd get mad again, but she just smiled mysteriously and said. "You'll see."

Soon we passed a dented sign with a picture of a stupid large, smiling fish: Munsonville. Population: 386. Everyone Welcome Here.

Yippee! (still sarcastic).

Well, if Shelby is cutesy pie, Munsonville ought to be good-bye and die. My first thought was, "ghost town with people." Main Street was a hard-packed dirt road. The sidewalks were plank. The buildings on the north side of the road were weathered brick and had painted wooden signs: Village Hall, Joe's General Store, Harper's Grocery, Dalton's Dry Goods, Walker's Apothecary, Munsonville Public Library.

On the south side was a lake, a dingy diner, and a row of really old fishing cabins. Beyond them, woods.

Aunt Silly pointed to an old building with a three-story turret.

"That's Munsonville Inn," she said. "Our home for two days."

"Is that the haunted house?" I asked.

She shook her head, drove to the back of the building, and parked. She opened the trunk, and we took out four bags. One was mine, one was hers, one was full of product, and one was full of stuff.

The front door was heavy. The inside was full of dark wood. The faded carpet had a viney design with pink flowers. Doesn't look anything like a werewolf lair.

The clerk was a fat woman with graying brown hair. Around her neck was one of Aunt Silly's necklaces. She had pasty skin and too much powder and red lipstick. Meaning, she looked like an oversized, slight burnt sugared jelly doughnut.

This pastry puff smiled when she saw Aunt Silly and said, "Welcome back, Priscilla."

Aunt Silly smiled, too, and said, "Thank you, Barbara." She signed the register and accepted the key. Hanging from the key was a tag: Room 307.

Then, miracle of miracles, Aunt Silly remembered I was with her.

"Barbara, this is my niece, Caryn. She's spending the summer with my brother and me. Caryn, this is Barbara Drake."

"Hi," I said.

"Are you having a nice summer?" the jelly roll asked.

"Eh," I replied.

Then Aunt Silly had to play peacemaker. "Caryn is a very talented writer. She's working on her first novel."

Miss Bismarck smiled, showing the lipstick on her teeth. Or maybe she was a werewolf and killed a couple of brats before work.

"How exciting," she said. "Is it a love story?"

"No, it's about a brutal werewolf who savagely massacres..."

And then fucking Aunt Silly had the gall to interrupt me!

208

"...check into our room now. Have a nice day, Barbara."

Aunt Silly rudely marched me to the elevator by my arm. So I rudely, and loudly, said, "I can walk by my fucking self!"

The doors to the musty, creaking, clanking dumbwaiter jerked its way to our beatific abode. Aunt Silly only gripped me tighter.

"Knock your shit off," Aunt Silly hissed from inside our unstable cubicle. "Or I'll send you to the woods."

I waggled my fingers in front of her face. "Oooo, I'm so scared."

Then she slapped me, Maggie, really fucking hard. The door opened. She pushed me out. And then grabbed my arm again, pinching it, and spat her words into my face: "You might get away with that shit at home. But you're not home now. Be miserable or happy; it's all up to you. But you WILL NOT be rude to my clients." She yanked my arm hard. "Got it?"

I jerked back, aghast that Aunt Silly could turn so spiteful. Maggie, I was really and truly speechless. I couldn't think of one line that would knock her into place.

In the meantime, she turned me around and jabbed a finger in my back. "Now go."

So I trudged down the hall with Aunt Silly poking me forward until we came to Room 304. She shoved me aside and unlocked it. The stupid room was as old as fuck. The white wallpaper was pale blue with salmon flecks, and it had peeled away in places. The beige carpet was worn, almost to the floorboards in some spots.

There was just one bed, yippee again. The bed was dark walnut and covered with a white-patterned quilt and blue pillows. Adorable.

A matching nightstand stood on either side of the bed. On each nightstand was a white lamp with a painted cornflower design. On the lamp were silver fixtures that reminded me of my free "werewolf" key.

A large dresser with a hanging mirror was across from the bed. On the dresser was a small television with large rabbit ears. So we could watch "telly" in bed. Dad and Aunt Silly didn't have "telly." I have a huge color console in my bedroom I never watch.

Near the bay window was a roll top desk with a high back chair.

The room smelled like old weeds, thanks to the glass bowls of dried brown petals on every empty space. I sniffed and said, "Hope it keeps the roaches away."

Aunt Silly laughed. "Wait and see."

Whatever was up her ass had melted. Let the fun begin!

"So where's the haunted house?"

"In the woods."

"What are we waiting for?"

"Lunch. Let's go."

And that, Maggie, is how I wound up at the old, dreary diner.

July 12

Dear Maggie

Aunt Silly and I had lunch at the only place in town to eat: Sue's Diner. For hick village that probably attracts amateurs scrounging for goldfish, the place was fucking packed with every type of man, woman, and child you could imagine.

Aunt Silly asked for a booth near the window. So, you know, I could admire the "view" through the fingerprints and toddler nose smudges on the glass. The vinyl blue-green set cushions were held together with cellophane tape. The gold-speckled tabletop was full of coffee stains.

A skinny woman a brunette ponytail led us to a booth near the window. Next her, a little boy who looked just like her, clasped two menus to his chest, which he had puffed out. But he didn't smile. He took his job that seriously. Poor kid. Not even old enough for school and already the shitty grownups in his life were exploiting him.

But the food in this shithole was terrific, actually. And we did not order hamburgers or cheeseburgers, ha ha.

We had a fish loaf with a cream sauce. We drank lemony iced tea. For dessert, Aunt Silly ordered something called "Steve's Chocolate Cake."

"Who the fuck is Steve?"

"A very nice man." Aunt Silly leaned forward and dropped her voice. "And you watch your mouth here. Steve and his parents ran this diner for many years. They are the best people."

"They're still running it?"

"No."

"Then who the fuck cares?"

"I care!" she hissed. "I care because these are my customers. You better learn some respect, or I'll send you to the woods!"

This time, Maggie, I felt a little concerned. Was Aunt Silly losing her mind? Did she have a stroke, an aneurysm, a brain tumor? Why did she quit being such a cool aunt? And what was in the woods that she kept threatening to send me there?

So I changed the subject until I could call Dad and let him know. I mean, she could be dangerous In her present state.

In the meantime, the skinny woman brought our cake. It was creamy and chocolatey. Aunt Silly said that's because the cake's made with sour cream and chocolate pudding.

"What's so fearsome about the woods?"

Aunt Silly slowly lowered her fork and looked at me as if I was the one who'd lost my mind. "Who said the woods are fearsome?"

"Oh, what the fuck! Why do you keep threatening to send me to the woods?"

"They're huge. You'd get lost and never come back."

Aunt Silly shoved the last piece of cake into her mouth. She beamed at me, showing chocolate smears on all her teeth.

I laughed out loud, and Aunt Silly
kicked me under the table.

But she was still grinning like a
wicked old witch with blackened teeth.

July 12
Dear Maggie,

After lunch, we headed to the
haunted house. To get to the haunted house,
we had to walk down dusty old unpaved
Main Street and into the woods.
As we walked, we smoked and talked.

"Is the house really haunted?" I asked
Aunt Silly. "Or are you just making it up?"

Aunt Silly shrugged and blew out
smoke. "Who knows? Everyone around here
says it's haunted."

She said the homeowner's name was
John Simons, and he just died a couple
years ago. He was a (so-called) famous
pianist and composer (I never fucking heard
of him). He married the minister's daughter,
built a mansion in the woods, and left town

after she and their kid died while she was pushing it out.

I guess it's sad. And it explained nothing.

But I humored her.

"So why do they think the house is haunted?"

"Lots of reasons," Aunt Silly said, crushing her cigarette under her foot without missing a step. "Mist. Shadows. Piano music." She jerked her head left. "We turn here."

It was a steep climb, especially after a heavy lunch. I wanted to mock her, honestly, Maggie, I really did. Those were stupid reasons for an entire village to be afraid of an old house.

But I kept my mouth shut. The whole time I walked up the hill with her, I felt like something was walking up right behind us. And I couldn't stop thinking about those three words.

Maggie, it was the way she said then together (Mist. Shadows. Piano music.) that gave me the creeps, just like thinking about The Clock Man.

Finally we reached the top of the hill, the longest, most uneasy walk of my life. The four-story house was nothing special or scary. It was old and gray and covered in green vines with pink flowers. It had lots of bay windows and a wrap-around porch.

Aunt Silly nudged me and pointed. "Look."

I looked. And looked. And looked Those damn viney flowers were everywhere. They wove themselves around the trees and the rest of the vegetation. They were literally everywhere.

It was so...weird. And unsettling.

It was almost as if the planter wanted to keep something out...or someone in.

Mist.

Shadows.

Piano music.

I turned to her and asked again, "Do you think it's haunted?"

Aunt Silly crossed her eyes and stuck out her tongue. But for a silly aunt, she still looked serious. "I think the world is full of things we can't explain." She poked me in the ribs and laughed. "Great place to let loose your Pandora's box, huh?"

"Dad told you?"

"Yep!"

I heard a rumbling in the distance and cocked my head.

"That's Steve, mowing the grass," Aunt Silly said. "He takes care of all the grounds."

"All of it?" I scanned the vast expanse (like how I phrased that, Maggie?). "And he takes care of his parents?"

"Yeppers. And he still helps out at Sue's Diner. I told you, Steve is true blue through and through and good as gold."

"People are mean and horrible and selfish."

"Not all people," Aunt Silly insisted. "And not Steve."

"I'll be the judge of that."

"Suit yourself."

Besides, Maggie, he sounds boring as shit.

July 12
Dear Maggie,

We spent the rest of the afternoon at Dalton's Dry Goods, the only place that stocks Aunt Silly's jewelry here.
The wooden floorboards groaned with every step. The owners looked tired. Mr. Dalton did stuff in the back. Mrs. Dalton haggled over the price of EVERY SINGLE FUCKING piece with Aunt Silly.

Their little girl looked about three. She sat in the corner on a blanket surrounded by plastic baby dolls and picture books. She had the same chestnut hair as her mother. She was squinting and turning the pages of a board book.

Three hours later I'd looked over every hand-embroidered blouse, every hand-stitched journal, all the hand-sewn clothes, every accessory that didn't come from Aunt

Silly, the yellowing postcards, the Montgomery Ward catalogue, and I had to pee super bad.

I glanced at the little girl. She had curled up on her blanket and fallen asleep, sucking her thumb.

"Do you have a bathroom?" I interrupted.

Mrs. Dalton opened her mouth to speak, and Mr. Dalton yelled out, "This ain't no service station!"

So I yelled back, "Do you want me to pee on your floor? Because that'll happen if..."

Aunt Silly pinched the back of my hand. Mrs. Dalton turned red and cleared her throat. "Sue's Diner has a public restroom."

I gave her my most simpering smile. "Thank you." And then I turned to Aunt Silly. "Mind if I take a walk?"

"No," she said. "I'll meet you in the lobby in an hour. Stick to the neighborhood."

So I waddled to Sue's Diner, which had "a public restroom." Meaning, just one. So I waited behind a young mom with three little girls who were jumping up and down with their hands between their legs. It took ten minutes for some man to come out. He was panting, sweating, and carrying a crumpled newspaper. Fucker.

Ten minutes after that, the woman came out, flustered, but no one had peed themselves. After taking a four-quart piss, I was heading out of the dump and to the neighborhood behind Main Street. This, too, was on a hill. I saw just three street signs: Pike, Blue Gill, and Bass.

Oh, fuck me!

Because the choices were so *irresistible*, I played eeny, meany, miney mo, and eliminated Pike and then Blue Gill. So up the steep gravely Bass Street I went, stretching my hamstrings to their limit.

The layout of the houses was odd. Near the bottom of the hill were tiny houses, scarcely bigger than the fishing

221

cabins. But as I climbed the hill, the size of
the houses grew larger and larger, until I
reached the telescopic three-story one at
the top right. To the left was an empty lot.
Beyond that, at the top of Blue Gill Road, I
glimpsed a large colonial.

Bass Street literally came to a dead
end.

Meaning it led into a cemetery with
lots of leaning tombstones. Curious, I
plodded in that direction and pushed past
the tall prickly grass, hoping to find
something useful for my werewolf story.

So with weeds scratching my legs, I
wandered through the forsaken place,
scanning names that meant nothing to me.
But Dad, and Aunt Silly, seemed certain I'd
find inspiration in this backwoods place, so I
kept meandering and pondering.

The cemetery merged with the woods.
I recalled Aunt Silly's words about the vast
size of these woods. I studied the tall old
trees, slowly turning around, to catch every
mesmerizing angle, so lush at the top they

seemed to be just one tree with many trunks.

And then I noticed something. Maggie, this is why Dad calls me a bloodhound. I noticed a broken stick on the ground near one of the trees. Beyond that, I some of the tall weeds hung at a bent angle, as if someone had snapped their little necks.

Impulsively, I pushed through these wild grasses. When I say "tall," Maggie I mean it. I was wading in weeds past my waist. Clouds of gnats attacked me, pissed I'd upset their sanctuary. I swatted their asses as I kept pushing my way through and then...

Well, then, Maggie, I found myself in the thick of the woods. The grass was trodden into the ground, as if someone, or a few someones, regularly walked this endless jungle of oaks and maple and pine and bracken.

A werewolf, maybe?

I checked my watch, but it was dead. I glanced at the sky, trying to gauge the time. Aunt Silly said one hour. I lost half of that waiting to pee and getting here.

I won't walk too far, I told myself. Just a little way. Just far enough to see where the path leads.

So I walked. Maggie, I walked for a long, long time. For a long time, that path had no end. And then it did.

Sort of.

The path ended at a crossroad. I could turn left, right, or keep straight ahead.

I stood in the middle of that crossroad, looking at woods in all directions.

Suddenly, I felt exposed. I was the only non-tree in a wide, open area. And I cast a very long, very visible, very dark shadow.

Mist.

Shadows.

Piano music.

A breeze muttered through the trees.

I felt cold and prickly. And just like when Aunt Silly and I were near the "haunted" house, I had the eerie sense of someone spying on me.

I whirled around; my shadow whirled, too.

And then I fucking tore off down the path. I ran and ran. Even when my side developed a stitch, I ran.

Holding onto my side, I plunged through all the tall weeds and through the cemetery, never stopping until I reached Bass Street.

I gasped and gulped and kneaded my side muscle. When the cramping subsided, and I could breathe through my strained lungs, I plodded down Bass Street to Munsonville Inn.

As I suspected, Aunt Silly was waiting for me in the lobby. She was flipping through a tattered magazine.

And then she said something that made me think she DID have a stroke. She said, "Well, that was fast."

"What?" I asked.

And then my heart jumped. My watch was ticking. Only ten minutes had passed since I left Sue's Diner.

THE FUCK???

Aunt Silly eyed my scratches.

"Any ideas for the "you know what?" she asked with a smile.

I nodded.

Maggie, I was too stunned to talk.

July 12,
Dear Maggie,

So after a bath and salve from Aunt Silly's "stuff" bag for my scratches, Aunt Silly and I went back to Sue's Diner for dinner.

It was late when we got there, so the dining room was nearly empty.
Steve Barnes was in there, so I finally got to meet him. He looked about twenty-six. He wore faded blue jeans, threadbare gym shoes, an apron over his blue T-shirt, and a hair net over his thick, blond hair.

He looked like a square awkward nerd, which he was. But he did seem genuinely friendly, and he made a perfect pizza pie for Aunt Silly and me. So I didn't tell him he fucked up with his mowing at the cemetery.

After dinner, Aunt Silly and I strolled along Lake Munson. The waves sloshed along the shore. The setting sun glowed red near the horizon.

I wondered what kind of fish, snails, plants, and spiders made this lake their home. I wondered how many of them had already died and become fish food...while the people wandering next to it sighed in pleasure about the peacefulness of the lake.

"Penny for your thoughts?" Aunt Silly said.

"Nope. You'll have to wait for the book to hit the stores."

She gave me a big smack on my ass.

Then she offered me a smoke.

For a person, she's all right!

July 13

Dear Maggie,

I sat up late last night writing ideas into my notebook while Aunt Silly smoked and watched television.

I slept like shit.

Aunt Silly tossed and turned a lot. This made the springs squeak like mice caught in traps by their tiny feet. Then just as I drifted off, she got up for her nightly piss, slamming the lid loud enough to wake the dead in the "haunted" house.

I'm surprised the other guests didn't charge down here to yell at her.

The next day, I stayed in the room writing. Aunt Silly visited with people she knew.

I did not go for a walk. Staying in this decaying old room by myself was eerie enough.

The whole time I was writing, I kept thinking about The Clock Man, the trees, the crossroad, and about *mist, shadows, and piano music.*

228

I kept turning around to make sure no one was in the room. I checked and rechecked the locks. I bought lunch from the refrigerated sandwich machine down the hall. That was OK because Aunt Silly and I got up late and had a big breakfast at Sue's Diner.

But even the hallways were strangely silent. In fact, the entire inn felt as quiet as a sealed tomb. No signs or sounds of life as I padded to the sandwich machine and back.

How loud was the clinking of the dime as it dropped into the metal box and the grinding of the gears as it dropped my lunch.

I snatched it and sped back to my room, turning locks and sliding bolts into place.

I leaned against the door, gasping. I thought of the twisty vines and pink flowers near the "haunted" house.

Was the "thing" outside my room?

Or had I just barricaded myself into its chambers?

Stupid, I told myself. You are so fucking stupid.

I marched across the room and grabbed a package of Ray's crispy chips, a package of Frisco's marshmallow sandwich cookies, and a can of Slurry's root beer from Aunt Silly' s stuff bag. I carefully arranged my hobo lunch on the desk.

Then I spent the rest of the day sipping, munching, and channeling my overactive imagination into the love story of Carrynne and Randy.

Maggie, I was so focused, I didn't even hear Aunt Silly when she walked into the room!

July 14
Dear Maggie,

Aunt Silly and I are back from Munsonville.

And the tabby with the tumor is back at Dad's office because it's dehydrated.

I was on my way out the door when Aunt Silly asked me to stop at one of the soap shoppes to drop off a couple of orders. Tourism is in full swing now, and none of the shoppes can keep Aunt Silly's jewelry in stock.

I'd help her twist wire and thread gems — honest — if I didn't have that werewolf story to write!

So while I was waiting for the owner, I gazed around the products near the counter. One jar of cream caught my interest, mostly because of the name: *Midnight Huntress*.

The label was pearlescent white with crisp black letters. I unscrewed the top and sniffed its shimmery insides. I was expecting vanilla or gardenia, but it actually smelled like a violet musk.

I vaguely remembered stories of witches rubbing themselves with the fat of unbaptized babies so they could ride to their sabbaths. And I wondered if Carrynne had a magic cream...could that help her get to Randy?

I mean, why NOT have a werewolf's mate using a magic ointment to get to her werewolf lover?

That and her magic clock to guide the time, of course. The thought stirred my imagination, like Rosie stirring enchanted herbs into her soup. I smiled because my werewolf story was becoming part of me, and I was becoming part of it. That has to make the ideas flow better, right, Maggie?

So I bought it, with Dad's bank card, of course.

Maggie, I couldn't rush to Dad's office fast enough. Seriously, I was pushing tourists and their greasy suntan oil aside to get there sooner.

"Wendy," I panted as soon as I burst through the door. "Quickly! I need pen and paper."

With a knowing grin, Wendy handed me both. I jotted down all my ideas, gave her the pen back and went to check on Tabitha, the actual name for the tabby, I found out.

When my book is published, Wendy gets a free autographed copy!

July 14

Dear Maggie,

So tonight after my shower, I tried the cream.

It glided easily over my skin and lightly scented me and the room with an earthy, floral, sensuous type of fragrance I can't really describe.

If it was a color, I'd say violet with sepia undertones. That's a good scent for a werewolf mate, isn't it?

After I absorbed the cream, I slowly slid my white nightgown over my head. And then I crawled under the covers with my notebook and pen.

I'm going to just lie here and pretend this ointment is transporting me to the boy in the basement.

I'm going to just lie here and pretend I'm Carrynne...and that her spirit is traversing the miles to be with her Randy.

He misses her so much! And she misses him!

And then I'm going to write the ideas in my head.

I am a midnight huntress!

July 15
Dear Maggie,

I woke up this morning plastered to my notebook and still drooling. Luckily, I could still make out some of the smeared words.

If no one needs me today, I'm going to write chapter five.

Please, please, please make no one need me today.

Please.

Please.

```
Chapter 5:
  "Magic Ointment"

I lie awake staring at the dark
sleek sky. I cannot fall asleep. I can
only think of Randy and his poor
infected paw.
Did the medicine get inside the house?
```

If the paw gets worse, will his paw fall off?

If he cannot run and hunt, will he die?

But finally I fall asleep with the key safely tucked beneath my pillow. In my dream, I float to Rosie's shoppe. She is stirring a bubbly soup the color of green phosphorescence.

As Rosie stirs, she sings:

"Take chamomile to beguile
"And sleep, sleep, sleep,
"Take Rosa Damascena
"Grow wiser than Athena
"And sleep, sleep, sleep
"Take lavender, you scavenger
"And sleep, sleep, sleep
"Take valerian, my canine heroine
"And sleep, sleep, sleep
"Take lemon balm, heal his palm
"And sleep, sleep, sleep
"Take passion flower, and within the hour
"You'll sleep, sleep, sleep"

From the center of the soup, a thick voice sang:

"Hink minx! the old witch winks,
"The fat begins to fry"

I wake up with a smile in the night. The fat. Of course.

I crawl out of bed and down to the kitchen. I open the refrigerator

235

door and look at the fat. I have lots of fat, two shelves of fat, creamy white and stored inside my mother's old canning jars.

I will not run out of fat soon. I get dressed and wait for the sun to rise.

After breakfast, I grab my mother's turquoise Italian raffia straw handbag from my mother's closet and put something in it.

Before I leave, I lay the rowan cane near the door before I lock it.

This is not as easy as it sounds. The cane was not by my door when I woke up, and the search for it was long and irritating. Finally, I found it. This time the cane was at the edge of the property, past the old gardens, and half buried by dead leaves. I wipe all the blood from the cane onto the grass, give that naughty cane a good spanking, and then carry it back to the door and set it in place. Then I pocket the key and hurry all the way to Rosie's. I push open the rusty metal door. A bell jingles. I sneeze against the dust.

Rosie is standing in the middle of the dark room, and she's stirring a cauldron.

"Whatcha makin' today, Rosie?" I ask, peering inside.

"Soup," Rosie grins.

I remove two jars from my mother's tote bag and place them on her wobbly wooden table. "I brought fat."

Rosie cackles happily. She sets down the ladle and picks up one of the jars. She unscrews the lid and sniffs. Then she nods and hands it back to me.

"It's powerful," she says.

"It's homemade," I say.

Rosie grabs an empty glass jar.

Then she starts taking bottles down off her shelves. One by one, she fills my jar with dried pinches of this and dried pinches of that.

She puts in tiny yellow-brown flowers and whole magenta-colored bulbs. She puts in light violet sprigs, chopped brown bits of root and two different kinds of brown-green flakes.

Rosie screws on the lid and shakes it up. Then she hands it to me. I put the jar of chamomile, Rosa Damascena, lavender, valerian, lemon balm, dried passion flowers into my mother's ugly handbag.

"Sleep," Rosie says.

"I will," I say back.

Rosie picks up her ladle and ignores the jars of fat on her table. Well, it's not my worry anymore. My only worry is Randy.

The door jingles behind me. I blink against the sunlight.

"Be patient, Randy," I say aloud. "I am coming soon."

Carefully, I carry my precious cargo home with me, but my arms quiver with the excitement. Soon, very, very soon.

When I get home, I set the handbag on the kitchen table and then go to the refrigerator. I take out a jar of fat and set it next to the handbag, so it has time to warm up.

Then I dash from room to room, making sure all the doors are locked and all the shades are pulled down, and all the curtains are drawn.

The house is dark and cool, but I can see fine. I go the cabinet for my mother's biggest mixing bowl. Then I open the drawer and take out a tablespoon. I place them on the kitchen table, where the bag still sits, waiting for me.

I unclasp the bag, take out the jar of Rosie's special blend, and carry it to the counter. I take off the sea green quilted cloth from my mother's three-speed blender. I shake the herbs into the blender, put the plastic lid on top, and push the button to high.

The loud whirrrrr fills the quiet house, but it's not as loud as my father's meat grinder. Mesmerized, I watch the plant corpses grind to a fine sage-green powder.

I switch off the blender and lift the plastic pitcher from the base. I bring the pitcher of powder back to the table.

I unscrew the jar of fat and dump the white glop into the bowl.

Then I pour the powdered blend into the bowl. With my spoon, I thoroughly mix the blend into the fat. I lean close to the bowl and inhale deeply.

Ahhhh!!!

I slide three fingers into my goop and squat, rubbing the gloop all over the tops of my feet and my soles. I cover each toe: top, bottom, and in-between.

Over and over I glide my fingers into the magic ointment. I cover my legs and work way up, coating my skin, and even my scalp, leaving my face for last

By now my head is swimming, and my eyes are drooping. The room wobbles and twirls. I feel my body sink to the floor as I slink out of it and waft out the door.

Traveling by spirit is much faster than traveling by body. I don't need the Rosie's moonstone because my spirit connects to Randy's spirit and knows the way. I soar over my backyard, the little stream that runs behind our property, across the hill and over the fields of tall grasses and wildflowers.

The cool wind blows across my body and whistles in my ears, but my thick layer of fragrant fat keeps me warm.

I'm approaching Randy's pitiful prison. I slowly ease to the ground, the descent gentler than a department store elevator, and land on my feet just in front of Randy's window.

I squat and peek inside. Randy is stretched out on the concrete, sound asleep. His clothes are tattered and torn.

I see the chink now, and the magic ointment lets glide through it. Noiselessly I float across the room until I reach Randy; I crouch beside him. About a foot away lies the package of herbs, waiting for me to apply them. I pick it up.

His straight brown hair, in wild disarray, partially covers his hard chest, which gently rises up and down with each breath.

His downy coat is matted with dried blood, and I see the slash marks in his fibrous arms and legs. His muscles resemble thick rope, even beneath the fur. One calloused hand covers his eyes.

Even injured, my Randy is a beautiful, breathtaking creature. And then I feel an invisible blow to my gut that almost makes me vomit.

I see Randy's other hand, his right hand, his injured hand. The hand is as blown up as a red birthday party balloon. Yellow sludge oozes from its pores.

"I'm too late," I sob out, dropping my talisman. "I'm too late."

My tears fall on Randy's cheeks, and he opens his eyes, his bewitching eyes of glowing green, and I'm drawn into their spheres, home at last.

He reaches up with his good hand and moves my hair away from the salty wet glop on my cheeks, the better to see me, his dear.

And he does see me. With his gaze, he paralyzes me.

His eyes move back and forth, searching me. I hold my breath, but I can still smell the sweat, the fat, the florals, the pungence.

We smell like the hunt.

Carrynne, I knew you'd come.

But I'm too late. I reach for the dirty sachet and hold it up. What good is a pittance for such a brutal wound?

He smiles. Even with his face creased with pain, he still smiles, softly, and my fears start to melt and drip herbal-scented fat onto his face.

Heal me, Carrynne.

Randy, how?

Heal me.

And so I do.

Snuffling and still crying, I untie the frayed gray ribbon on Rosie's old linen bag and pat the herbs onto Randy's hand. It takes a few tries because his hand is so engorged, they slide off.

But my own hands are still full of fat, so that makes the healing herbs stick to his hand. It takes a long time because they stick to my hand, too. I pat as gently as I can,

but it's not gentle enough. He winces,
but he does not moan or cry out.

Then I squat beside him to study
his hand and wait for healing. But
healing doesn't come.

Randy chuckles softly.

Come lie beside me, Carrynne.

I shake my head.

*No, Randy. I want to watch the
healing. I cannot rest while you are
maimed.*

Aren't you my mate?

*Yes, Randy. I'm your mate
forever.*

Then lie with me and rest.

*I am resting, Randy. My body is
sleeping on my kitchen floor.*
*I know. Rest on me. Tonight we go
together.*

My heart leaps inside me with a
joy that touches the sky. With the
syllables of "tonight" and "we" and
"together" reverberating throughout my
fat-soaked spirit, I lay my head on
his warm hide and let his heartbeat
soothe me to sleep.

July 16

Dear Maggie,

Tabitha, the tabby with the tumor,
died in my arms today.

While Dad was listening to its little heart and lungs with his stethoscope, it just gave a little sigh and was gone.

I can't write anything today.

I'm staying in my room with the door that won't close and keeping a pillow over my head.

July 17
Dear Maggie,

Aunt Silly took a long time at the leather shoppe today, so long that I wound up trying on a midi leather coat.

I never really cared for leather, but today I needed to touch something that wasn't furry like a cat. As I ran my hand down the length of the coat, I felt carnal urges in my fingertips that I couldn't describe. It was like I had an animal nature inside me that wearing this coat woke up. It was like my fingers had hard-ons and that some...force...was driving them to hurt, maim, destroy. Nothing would satisfy them except ripping into other humans until they spurted out blood.

Of course, sweltering in a leather coat in the middle of July contributed to that sense, I'm sure! Tourists: they will buy fucking anything with an inflated price tag and the word "exclusive" scrawled on it.

Maggie, I was so mesmerized with stroking that coat that Aunt Silly had to say my name three times before I saw her standing in front of me.

Sheepishly (get it?), I slid out of the coat and hung it back up.

"Sorry," I said, actually blushing. "It's for…"

Aunt Silly put her finger to my lips and winked. "Don't give bystanders your ideas."

She's great, Maggie. She really is!

July 18
Dear Maggie,

Got a bad summer cold.

Fever, shaking, chills, nausea.

Aunt Silly keeps taking my temperature with a mercury thermometer, and I fade into dreams of molten moons.

I dream of running across hills with my werewolf mate.

I sip canned chicken broth. It's full of tiny, pressed squares of fake chicken meat and slippery noodles.

My worried dad hovers over me. His hand is gentle. He's kind and compassionate.

No wonder animals love him. No wonder that...

July 19
Dear Maggie,

The flexible obese waist gave an astonishingly superior catch to the ethical marbles that applied the fantasy critic in jest and in broken context.

The dress is in the reservoir to roll and soak.

July 20

Dear Maggie

I'm feeling a little better today. Was really out of it yesterday.

Aunt Silly even spent half a day scrubbing out the tub so I could take a hot bath and ease my aching muscles. They hurt so much, as soon as the warm water engulfed them, I thought I'd puke. But I breathed it back, and the lurching passed.

As I soaked, my mind wandered to the boy in Gordon James' basement. Is this how he feels, all cold and achy and sick on the floor?

Is he OK? What if he's not OK? How will I finish the story?

And if I don't finish the story, what will happen to Carrynne and Randy?

The thought jabs me with paroxysms of lovesickness. I actually begin to cry, Maggie, as in sobbing hard out loud, which I tried to hide by turning it into a cough.

That caused Aunt Silly to call out,

"Caryn, are you OK?"

"Yes," I called back.

No, Aunt Silly, I am not OK, but I don't speak the words aloud.

Here in your serendipity little town, the eminent bank president is keeping a naked boy hostage in his basement. And I'm keeping his dirty secret for the sake of literature and art.

But only for a little while. When my werewolf love story is written, I am going to the police!

July 21
Dear Maggie

Better, but drained.

Planning to say home, rest, write chapter six, and nap lots.

Weird dreams lately, the kind a sick person gets.

But I'm a writer. So I took notes.

July 22
Dear Maggie,

If I hadn't been sick, I don't think I could have written a chapter this brilliant.

I must confess, it's so good, I'm a little in awe of it.

I think you will be, too.

Chapter 6:
"Liquid Silver"

I wake up naked on the hard kitchen floor, sweating and shivering, and clutching my knees, which I've drawn up to my breasts.
Even though the house is still sealed like a tomb, the blinding sun radiates through the blocked windows, brightening the dark room with unwelcome light.

My head pounds like a jackhammer, and my mouth is wadded with stuffing from an old bloody pillow. My stomach leaps and dives; I shudder against each wave of nausea. Every muscle is stretched or torn, and the thought of moving fills me with deep dread.

But I can't lie here forever. I'm too damaged, and I know it.

So I let go of my knees and raise up to one elbow, pausing as pain blazes through all four limbs, and I fight back against the strong urge to vomit. The fat has seeped into my skin, but I'm so marred by scratches and cuts, I can hardly admire the supple bits among the torn ones.

248

When I can stand, I will soak in the tub.

An hour later, I am sitting. An hour after that, I am standing. I gingerly take a step and yelp. I freeze, breathing hard – and then take another. Finally I hobble to the bathroom and turn on the faucets. I watch the steam rise from the hot waters, and I think about chinks in walls and werewolf spirits.

When the tub is half full, I lower myself into its depths and allow the water's warmth to cool my open sores and my painful muscles. The water smarts and turns pink from all the dried blood, but I resist the smarting, and let the heat do its job while my mind rewinds to last night's magical lunacy.

It began, I remember, on the floor of the lair. With a contented sigh, I sink further into my manmade pool until the tap water sloshes my chin. I lay my head against the cool back of the tub and gaze up at the crack in the ceiling.

Not even a crack can stop me or keep me out. Not anymore.

I am there...

Even before I open my eyes, I hear the deep sighs of animal breathing. I smell musk and feel the warmth of his pelt against my cheek. My naked bones ache from the cold concrete, and I tremble, despite my layer of fragrant fat. I feel tugs on my scalp as Randy's fingers slowly, methodically comb through my hair. I bury my face in his fur, and my trembling with cold becomes trembling with anticipation.

My Randy is awake. I am ready. So I open my eyes.

I see a semi-dark room illuminated by a green calcite glow, and a vague craving stirs inside me. The moon's call thumps in his chest and beats through mine. I sense the familiar calling of my name, but it calls from inside Randy and nowhere else, and I now know it wasn't the moon, it was never the moon, that ever called my name, unless the moon was more than a moon.

My fingertips tingle, and prickles creep up my legs; I squirm with restless, surging energy.

I feel the scrape of claws across my neck and down my spine. A growl roars in my ear, and I nearly burst with the need to bite and tear.

Ready, Carrynne?

Yes, Randy.

We explode, leaving our humanity on the floor, and blast through the chink, trampling down the fields - fields that took me hours on foot - in three pounces and charging up the hill like mad wildebeests until we reach the top, where the sky encloses us like heavy dark theater curtains. The world is ours, and it's our stage. The scene is set for death, and we give a performance no one will live to remember.

Nothing escapes our hunger; their screams clang in my ears, and their flesh, still warm with blood, satisfies a need beyond food.

Overhead, the silver moon is molten and melting. I think of rainy afternoons at my bedroom window, watching streaks trickle paths. Yes, this is what I think as the moon's viscous fluid oozes down; a childhood that was never simple or innocent, a childhood that was now, thankfully, gone.

I know you killed them, Carynne. You killed them with mercury poisoning.

A flashback of me, under the spell of the moon, gliding from bedroom to bathroom and silently opening the old metal medicine chest without so much as a single creak.

I move aside my father's aftershave that smells disgustingly of bergamot for the one tool that always decided fate: sick or well.

Tonight, we are all sick.

And then I slink into their bedroom and break the mercury thermometer under their noses while they sleep, the quicksilver balling onto their skin and rolling away.

The moon, you see, was hungry - and begging to be fed.

I didn't need parents anyway. And their hamburger kept me fed for as

long as it lasted, and the fat off
their bones kept me warm tonight.

I laugh aloud, a rich, metallic
laugh, and my claws tear up clumps of
grass, and the sweet earth delights my
nostrils as I sniff the dirt straight
up to my brain. This and the smell of
death excites me more than any drug,
so we speed across the endless hill,
devouring anything that gets in our
way.

On and on, and on, and on, and
on we bound, two of a kind, a pack of
two.

Under a dripping mercurial moon.

July 23

Dear Maggie,

So once again I'm out of fucking ideas.

Shit, I almost wish I was sick again
just to get them flowing.

What I needed to do was sneak to
Gordan James' house again.

So today I did just that.

I told Aunt Silly I was taking a short
walk.

She asked if I was feeling up to it.
And then the phone rang.

Yes, I was literally "saved by the bell."

No need to scout out Dad's schedule. He wasn't expecting me.

So I acted as if I was taking an aimless stroll and that I, somehow, wound up on Fifth Street. And I meandered some more until I arrived at 666, where I quickly slunk to the hedge and disappeared on the other side.

Across the lumpy ground I crawled, a bit breathless, with my recent illness. As I crawled, I panicked, some. What if he wasn't there? What if he was? What if he needed help now, today, and I had to get the police? How would I finish the world's greatest werewolf love story if I couldn't see him?

But soon I was peering through the bubble glass. The naked wolf boy was lying still, and he was still chained to a spike in the concrete by leg cuffs.

His brown hair was still long, matted, and wild. He still didn't look hungry, tired, or sick, even though he was still covered with red splotches and blisters.

And this time, Maggie, I really do think he recognized me...and was happy to see me.

It seemed as if his green eyes lit up, a little, and he sort of smiled, just a slight curving of his lips and a bit of pleasure on his face.

He lay relaxed and carefree, as if he was in the basement by choice. But he couldn't be there by choice, could he?

I "came to" when my head smacked against the window. I started to yell, "Ow!" and then remembered where I was. I strained to see through the bubble glass. The wolf boy had gone to sleep.

I scrambled out of the yard as best as I could. I was shaking, and twilight was descending. I tried to hurry, thinking Aunt Silly would be frantic.

But when I got back to the house, Dad wasn't home yet, and Aunt Silly was talking to a customer. I waited in the doorway, actually clutching the jamb, until she hung up.

"Aunt Silly," I warbled, "I think I need food."

I must have looked pretty gray. Because she took one look at me and zoomed across the room for the tub of chocolate ice cream and a spoon.

"That'll revive you pretty quickly," she said.

I sank to floor, scooped up a mouthful, and slowly sucked it off the spoon, thinking about Randy with every suck.

Aunt Silly picked up the phone and ordered pizza. All by herself.

July 24
Dear Maggie,

I couldn't sleep, not with a head full of story.

So I stayed up to write the next chapter.

And then I fell asleep with the moon in my mind.

Chapter 7
"Where Does Your Garden Grow"

Every night the moon is full,
thanks to Peter Stumpp, my clock
friend from The Clock Man.
So every night I hunt with Randy.
But every morning, I wake up in my
bed. I don't know why. I don't
remember how.

I leave the house right away,
dressed only in a thick layer of fat.
I don't eat crunchy cold cereal
anymore. The only crunchy things I eat
are bones: animal bones and human
bones.

Soon I'm gliding to Randy's den.
My key stays under my pillow because
my house is still locked from the
inside out. I'm traveling by wolf
spirit, no keys needed.

I have not seen the rowan cane
for days. I hope the cane is happy and
enjoying plenty of cane-style
escapades.

I skim over my backyard, the
little stream that runs behind our
property, my hill and the fields. I
gaze down at the scratchy thick
grasses, daisies, black-eyed Susans,
clover, and Queen Anne's Lace. I
delight in the pungent air and the
chirring of dark clouds of insects all
around me and sticking to my fat.

This is always the longest part
of twenty-four hours, the time I'm
away from Randy.

Finally the forlorn house emerges, and I know paradise is not far away. Two sets of wolf tracks lead straight to the back yard and stop at a basement window.

I slip through the chink, and Randy is waiting. His green eyes flash when he sees me. I sink to the ground, and he sinks with me, and takes my face into his warm tanned hands. Soft hair, like the hair on his face, covers the backs and knuckles. I cup my hands over his, happy neither hand is swollen anymore.

Rosie's medicine fixes things that are swollen. Today I am glad I left it at home.

I reach out with one hand to touch the hair on his cheek. It's soft, like down.

Carynne, he growls, the breath of each syllable a warm wind on my lips.

I'm shaking with a strange desire, but I am unafraid, and I am ready to receive my Randy.

I open my mouth.

He draws me close and probes my mind with gleaming eyes.

My knees tremble, but I can't look away.

Randy…

His lips are like worn leather, and they touch mine with the tenderest of kisses, and I kiss him back before I realize I'm kissing him.

His hands glide to my neck; he holds it in place; he possesses it. Each kiss, each ravenous nip, lands exactly where Randy intends it to land, and he seals it with a grunt or a moan.

The only solid part of my world is Randy and my head. The rest of me has turned to quivery, quaking, slippery gelatin, like a forgotten molded dessert on a paper plate at a summer picnic.

He kisses me until I am bruised and raw, and still he kisses me, even while I'm smashing into him with staccato kisses of my own.

His hair mingles with mine, and his flesh blends into my flesh on the kitchen floor, and Randy's kisses are my kisses, an eternity of kissing.

I am marked with kissing. They are Randy's marks, from him to me. And I like it a lot.

Later, after we hibernate, after we hunt, and after we feast, we lie together on top of the hill under a brilliant golden moon. My stomach bulges with spoils, and Randy's hand clasps mine, a firm reminder of where I belong.

After a long, long while, he speaks.

You have to remove the aconite, Carrynne.

I turn toward him. It's very dark, but I can clearly see my Randy.

Like me, Randy is flat on his back, beguiled by the magnetic light of the night. His eyes are luminescent and hazy, as if under a spell; his lips are slightly parted.

I rise up on one elbow and trace his lips with a finger. He playfully tries to bite it, but I jerk away. His dazed look vanishes, and he gives me a crooked smile.

Silly Randy. How can I remove the aconite when I don't know where it is?

In my mind, I already have the answer. I will see Rosie tomorrow. I will ask Rosie to make a charm for me so I can find what I cannot see.

With a claw, Randy lightly, so lightly I can scarcely perceive it, traces my face. He starts at my forehead and proceeds counterclockwise. His claw glides and slides, turns and twists, and I realize it's dancing. His claw is dancing widdershins on my face.

The cane.
The cane?
Yes.
He smiles broadly now.
The cane. You still have it?
How did you know about the cane?
I felt it.

He brushes my hair off my face – his claws are nearly retracted now – and gazes at me so intently that I wish he'd gaze at me forever.

Felt it?

Carrynne, are we not mates?

I nod, my speech swallowed up by intensity of crystal green. The moon is large and bright. His eyes are small and sharp. The moon and his eyes are different, but they are the same. Bring them together, and they work magic.

He inches closer, and I'm hungry. I can't move, and I can scarcely breathe, but I can eat.

And then, he says as he moves in for the kill. He draws out the moment and notes my quivering with a satisfied smile. *And then you'll burn the cane.*

Burn the cane? Silly, Randy, why would I burn the cane?

But even before I form the words, I know in my heart I'll do it. Find the aconite, burn the cane: these are simple requests, almost too simple for one who easily killed the owner of the cane.

Only…I wonder how long it will take me to find the cane this time.

Do it, he says.

He pounces. A little cry of delight escapes my throat.

And then he pins me down and silences the cry.

July 25

Dear Maggie,

I'm so excited!!!!

The greatest werewolf love story the world's ever seen is almost written!!!!

Just three more chapters and then...fame! fortune!

And then I'll avenge "you know who."

I can't share the details of my plans because it's too dangerous for anyone to know.

I know you won't tell on me, Maggie. But it's best not to leave a written record.

But believe me when I say I'm working on my strategy.

I owe it to "him," don't you think?

July 26
Dear Maggie,

Walls lean.

Shadows lengthen.

Dad and Aunt Silly whisper a lot more.

My life is a room of distorted mirrors.
Nothing has changed.
But something is off.

July 27

Dear Maggie,

So Wendy quit!

Dad never mentioned it. Maybe that's why he and Aunt Silly have been whispering so much. He's worried about how he will get all the work done without her.

See why I don't like people? Stupid cunt just up and left!

"No she didn't," Dad said quietly as he picked up a chart. "I knew she was leaving at the end of September. She's getting married."

"Married? What the fuck, Dad? How come I didn't know this?"

Dad closed the chart and picked up the next one. "Did you ask her?"

"Did I walk in here every day saying, 'Hey, Wendy, just checking. Planning on getting hitched any time soon?' No Dad, I fucking didn't. And in case you haven't noticed, it's not fucking September, either!"

But Dad didn't look up. "Her mom got sick. She had to leave early to take care

262

of her. She might even postpone her wedding."

His face drooped, like a puppy who wet the carpet. "I'm not happy about it, either, Carrynne. We worked very well together. Now I'll have to train someone new."

"What's her address? I want to send her a card."

He raised his eyes. "Caryn Alaina, drop it."

Dad had never spoken curtly to me. He must be really upset.

And so, Maggie, I dropped it.

July 28
Dear Maggie,

And this is how a werewolf story stalls.

By dividing my time helping Aunt Silly and Dad.

Especially since the moon is full, and he's hobbling around on his rowan cane.

Fuck.

July 29

Dear Maggie,

Dad is sick.

He has a fever, and he's coughing a little.

Dad is never sick. Aunt Silly said she's probably next.

"That's how these viruses work," she said. "They just run through the household."

Today he was sick enough to close up shop early, come home, and go right to sleep on the couch!

July 30

Dear Maggie,

Dad slept almost all day on the couch.

He shivered under the blanket even though the day was warm, even though no breeze blew through the window.

He had me go down to the shop and tape a special note on the door. The note said he would be closed Monday.

And he had me call his appointments, cancel them, and then give them numbers to his colleagues in Jenson and Thornton.

People were disappointed, but they understood. That's how much they like my dad.

All of them asked me to give him little well wishes. For people, that was really nice of them.

Except I never did tell him.

Because he never woke up long enough to hear them.

Poor Dad.

July 31
Dear Maggie,

Walk with me. I'm so scared and upset, I'm shaking.

I had taken a break from my werewolf story and wandered into the kitchen for an afternoon snack. Aunt Silly was sitting at the kitchen table, twisting wire. She didn't have the radio on, and the room felt oddly silent.

"Where's Dad?" I asked.

"He had a vet emergency," she said absently.

Maggie, this is why I love my dad so much. Even when he's sick himself and should be resting in bed, he gives up his bed for me and sacrifices himself to help a helpless animal.

"I'm going for a walk," I said.

Aunt Silly just nodded.

"I'm grabbing a smoke," I said.

And then she nodded again.

So I slid a cigarette out of the pack, lit it, and shut the door behind me. I thought as I sucked in and sucked out. It must be a resident, I surmised. Only a resident would know where to find Dad if he wasn't at the office.

I didn't recall hearing the telephone ring. But then again, I was very into my werewolf love story. When I write, it's almost like I'm transported into the very words. I twist to their shape, their characters, and become part of the fabric of the page. It's that absorbing.

I throw the butt on the ground (yeah, I'm a terrible litterbug) and pick up my pace. It's easy to do because the tourists start to thin out after two o'clock...and definitely by three. And it was later than that.

When I got to Dad's office, everything looked closed up. Now I didn't expect him to raise all the blinds and turn the "closed" sign to "open."

But I did expect a sense of activity and movement. The office felt as shut up as when Dad locked it early on Saturday.

So, please, Maggie, take this walk with me. Because I am alone and scared. Here we go!

I slide my key inside the lock.

I turn the tumbler.

I hear the click. I push the door open.

"Dad?"

I snap on lights.

"Dad?"

Strange.

Aunt Silly seemed certain he was here.

No sounds except my sneakers squeaking on the waxed tile.
But Dad is sick. Maybe he fainted. Or had a heart attack in one of the rooms.
So I check each exam room.

No sounds.

Just my hissing breath.

Just my drumming heartbeat.

Just the ocean roaring in my ears.

"Dad?"

I check the supply room. And the surgical room. And the boarding room.

Nothing.

Finally, I have only one room to check.

Dad's office.

Only the office is left.

The door is ajar.

Ajar with sunlight stripes across the floor.

"Dad?"

Is he in there?

Is he hurt?

I've never gone into Dad's office, except when he's there. Because I love and respect him that much.

But I do it anyway.

Because, you know, just in case.

And then I started having weird flashes of remembrances.

"Oh, grandmother, what big ears you have!"

"All the better to hear you with."

"Oh, grandmother, what big eyes you have!"

"All the better to see you with."

"Oh, grandmother, what big hands you have!"

"All the better to grab you with!"

"Oh, grandmother, what a horribly big mouth you have!"

"All the better to eat you with!"

I tippy toe, panting anxiously, right up to the threshold.

I peer around the door.

"Dad?

Empty.

And in order.

As it should be.

Except...

Except the top, left-hand drawer of Dad's desk.

It's slightly open.

As if my tidy, precise Dad left in a hurry.

A dad who never leaves open drawers has left a drawer open in his office.

It hurts to breathe.

I felt like I was standing at the bottom of a fiery pit, where a chute sent down memories, one after the other, until I became engulfed in memories, and, and...

OH, GOD, MAGGIE, IT HURT SO MUCH TO BREATHE!!!

"I can't breathe," I giggle and gasp.

Dad keeps tickling me and singing, "Who's afraid of the big bad wolf..."

Maggie, I had to do it. I had to force one foot in front of the other.

"Presently a wolf came along and knocked at the door, and said, 'Little pig, little pig, let me in, let me in!'"

"Daddy, why does the wolf want in?"

Aloud, I chanted, "The drawer, the drawer. The answer's inside the drawer."

Dad was gone, and the answer was inside the drawer. But did I want the answer?

I put one foot in front of the other.

"Write a story, Caryn."

"What shall I write, Daddy?"

"The best werewolf love story in the whole wide world."

I'm at the desk. The drawer is empty. Almost.

"What are you drawing, Mouse?" Dad teased. "Werewolves."

I shook my head. "You have to guess."

Dad grinned. "No werewolves?"

"You have to guess."

Dad gave a sigh of pretend irritation. "Shoot, Mouse."

271

Way in the back, I see a wad of clear plastic wrap.

"A werewolf that's a Martian?"

An ordinary wad of plastic wrap in a tidy man's left-open drawer.

"No, Dad."

I reach for it and, as if bidden by an unseen power, look up — and out.

Somehow, my gaze draws to the window and out to the tiny patch of grass.

Let him in, Caryn! Let the big bad wolf IN!"

There they stand, about three feet tall, the row of them, in the half shade of the late afternoon, way in the back of the yard of Dad's office.

Rooted on yellow-green stalks.

Teeny white eyes staring at me through their purple hoods.

With my hand on the wad, I return their stare.

Yellow green stalks.

Teeny white eyes.

Hooded petals.

Purple.

Blue.

Aconite.

AUGUST

August 1

Dear Maggie,

There's a melancholy in August I can't describe.

Almost as if my spirit senses the dying summer and silently mourns the loss.

Only in summer I'm free.

Even a desire for completing my werewolf story is ebbing As soon as I think, "Hey, I should finish it," my mind arches away, like a snake prepared for attack.

So I don't force it.

Even though I'm grounded and have all the time in the world!

August 2

Dear Maggie,

So like I said, I'm grounded.

Worse, I've disappointed Dad.

When he caught me, hand in his drawer, all he said was, "Caryn, I'm so disillusioned."

He moved my hand, pulled out the wad, and held it up.

Dried purple flowers and brown tubers.

"Aconite," Dad said. "Wolfsbane. Deadly in large amounts, relieves anxiety in small doses."

I hung my head.

My dad, my wonderful, caring, compassionate dad who prized only the best for his clients, grew his own wolfsbane to keep them calm.

I've never felt more ashamed.

"Dad," I stammered. "I...I don't know what to say."

"I do." Dad put the aconite back in the drawer and shut it. "You're grounded."

August 3
Dear Maggie,

I need direction. I've never disappointed dad.

I feel awful.

August 3

Dear Maggie

I have GOT to go see him.

I have a hunger for him I can't describe.

But I can't go anywhere until my punishment is done.

I don't have to stay in my room. I can still help Aunt Silly, and I do. Although she was pretty frosty for the first day or so, she's over it.

But help at Dad's office? Nope.

Aunt Silly is out delivering orders by herself.

I'm pacing the tiny house like a caged beast.

Or like Randy.

Or like Gordan James' prisoner.

Whom I can't go see.

Fuck this summer.

August 4

Dear Maggie,

I'm still in prison.

In case anyone cares.

I know you do.

August 5

Dear Maggie,

I'm so bored and broken in spirit, I have to do something.

I need to work on my werewolf love story. But I can't go see the wolf boy.

And every time I think about my werewolf love story, I think about the aconite and…and…

Maybe I'll write some more of my short werewolf stories. I know they're not very good stories.

But if I don't do something, Maggie, I'll…I'll…

I'll lose my mind!!!

August 5

Dear Maggie

So here's the story I wrote today. It's not fascinating, like Carrynne's and Randy's story.

But it is mine.

Erika Cusatelli is a new teacher at one-room school that sits on top of a very high hill. The hill is so tall and so steep that Erika and all the children are hoisted up to the hill by ski lifts.

No one in the town of Heigh Ho know why the school was built on top of a hill. Or why all the children were in the third grade.

"It's tradition," all the locals say whenever anyone asks them the reason. "We've always done it this way."

The people of Heigh Ho are very traditional people. They live in traditional little houses with a garden patch in front and a charcoal grill in the back. Everyone owned a dog or a cat or a bird or a goldfish or a turtle. They all have fences, not to keep anyone out, but so dads can pause in their grass cutting duties to lean over the fence and talk with their neighbors. And the moms can do the same when they hang up the laundry to dry.

Still, it's extremely inconvenient for Erika and all thirteen of her students to get to the top of the hill every day. Some days Erika wishes the school board had shared this little detail before she agreed to the job.

Then again, maybe not. Erika was desperate for the job, a detail she,

too, did not share with the school
board.

Erika was a werewolf.

Now Erika did not like being a
werewolf. In fact, she really, really
hated being a werewolf.

The reason Erika kept losing all
her jobs is because she kept eating up
all her students and their parents.

Every month at the new moon,
Erika had a new job.

Every month after the full moon,
Erika was once again out of a job.

Erika hated living this way.
Being out of work so much was hard to
pay all her bills on time.

And yet, Erika really liked
teaching third grade She loved her
students, all of them. And even though
she never kept any of them for very
long, she always remembered their
names.

Like Davey, who struggled with
math.

And Lenore, who was already
reading at the fifth grade level.

And JoJo, who wanted to be a
weatherman and had a collection of
antique thermometers.

Teaching third grade was lots of
fun for Erika. The kids were old
enough to work independently, and yet
they were still young enough to stay
juicy with every bite.

But because the kids were too
young to stay alone, Erika was the
first person up the ski lift in the

morning and the last person to ride down the bucket at night.

And Erika always let her students know it was safe to come up because she tied a little yellow scarf to the ski bucket before she set it back down.

One Friday night just before the full moon, as Erika locked up the little schoolhouse for the night and prepared to ride down the bucket, she noticed a set of giant, muddy footprints just outside the schoolroom door.

The footprints looked as if they were made by someone wearing heavy boots. But the strange thing about these footprints is that they did not lead anywhere.

They did not go up the hill.

The did not go down the hill.

They did not go around the schoolhouse.

It was just one set of heavy muddy boot prints pointing toward the door of Erika's little schoolhouse, as if the wearer of those boots appeared without warning on the stoop and then vanished out of sight.

Now, if there's something a child-eating werewolf cannot tolerate, it's an empty mystery.

And as a third grade teacher, Erika knew that, logically, those boot prints belonged to someone.

So Erika decided to wait.

She waited all Friday night.

She waited all Saturday. And all Saturday night.

And all Sunday. And all Sunday night.

On Monday morning, the ski bucket did not come down for the children.

So Mr. Rutgers, the head of the school board, asked the ski lift operator to send the bucket down. The bucket was empty. Erika's yellow scarf was not tied to it.

By now, a crowd had gathered.

"I'm going up," Mr. Rutgers announced. "I'm going up to check."

The townspeople waved encouragement to him as the bucket slowly rose in the air. Mr. Rutgers looked down and waved back, smiling.

When he reached the schoolhouse, he noted the boot prints on the porch. He did not see Erika.

So he took out his key and unlocked the door. When he stepped inside, he saw everything was in order, right down to the pile of hair on the floor.

Mr. Rutgers got the broom and dustpan, swept up the hair, and threw it on the stove, where he burnt it up.

Then he put the broom and dustpan away, locked the schoolhouse, and picked up the fake boot prints on the porch.

Then he rode back down on the bucket, waving the boot prints in the air amidst the cheering of the crowds.

"School's canceled today," Mr.
Rutgers told the children.

"Hip, hip hooray!" all the
children cheered.

Then they went home to watch
television.

Mr. Rutgers went to his office,
picked up the phone and began to dial.

"Sam," he said to the man on the
other end of the line. "We just
starved another werewolf. Please send
a replacement right away."

Maggie, I just want to cry.

August 6

Dear Maggie

Wanna know how pathetic I am?

I called Mom today.

Aunt Silly had, get this, actually took
out the trash all by herself. A neighbor was
outside trimming her hedges and the two
got to talking.

Maybe it's because the sun is shining,
and my spirit is grey.

Maybe it's because I've let Dad down,
and I need a Mom.

Do you have a Mom, Maggie? Was she
a card-playing, chain-smoking boozer, or

was she the starched aprons, homemade chocolate chip type?

Does it really matter — as long as the love is there?

Whatever the reason, I called. The phone rang and rang and rang and rang.

I hung up crying.

August 6
Dear Maggie,

Lying in bed listening to the rain.
It sounds sad, I think.

August 7
Dear Maggie

It's still raining today.

It'd be a great day to start wrapping up the world's greatest werewolf love story.

Except I fucked that up, I guess.

August 8
Dear Maggie

*I wrote another werewolf short story.
Might as well, right?*

Tanya O'Toole quickly tied her shoes and headed outside for her morning run, Dawn was just breaking over the horizon in pink and orange, and the air was light and fresh and cool with early spring. It was her favorite time of the morning.

The neighborhood was quiet, except for maybe the occasional bark of the dog in the distance. Soon, the area would come alive with milkmen delivering the days milk, and husbands leaving for work, and children boarding school buses, and mothers waving good-bye and handing off lunchboxes.

Tanya stretched a few times and did a few jumping jacks. Then she strolled down the front walk to the sidewalk, increasing her speed every few paces until she broke out into a brisk jog.

On and on and on Tanya jogged past one brick bungalow after the other. She turned the corner and continued on her merry way, the tune of an old song she heard on the radio this morning replaying in the back of her mind.

Tanya rounded the corner and kept jogging.

She hoped her boss would not be too surly today. Merle Jones didn't have the mildest personality, but he was generally fair. Lately, though, he was moody and short-tempered. That made working as his personal secretary at the T.R R. Nelson Insurance Company very, very tense.

Tanya came to a crossroad and waited for a car to cross. The driver wore a coat with a collar up high and a hat with the brim down low. As the car slowly moved through the intersection, the driver turned to look at her. Its face was a grinning skeleton. Its eyes were empty sockets.

She gasped and shrank back.

The car drove away.

Tanya ran across the intersection on shaking legs and found all the bungalows had disappeared. She was now running across an open field. She turned and looked over her shoulder. The bungalows were still there. She looked ahead. Nothing but open fields.

Each time Tanya looked back, the houses looked smaller. Finally Tanya was so far away, she could not see a single house. Tanya ran so far and so long, she ought to be tired. But the more Tanya ran, the more energy grew inside her.

Finally Tanya touched her hands to the ground and ran on both her hands and feet, on and on and on and on…

With a groan, Tanya rolled over in bed and silenced her alarm clock.

She hated getting up, but it was the only way to get a nice run before driving to work downtown.

She quickly got dressed, gulped a glass of juice, tied her shoes, and headed out to the front porch. Dawn was just breaking over the horizon in pink and orange, and the air was light and fresh and cool with early spring. It was her favorite time of the morning.
The neighborhood was quiet, except for maybe the occasional bark of the dog in the distance. Soon, the area would come alive with milkmen delivering the days milk, and husbands leaving for work, and children boarding school buses, and mothers waving good-bye and handing off lunchboxes.

But she, Tanya, would be long gone. She did this every morning; she knew the routine.

It wasn't easy being a secretary to a werewolf, especially to a werewolf that wasn't nocturnal and liked early morning prey.

But it was Tanya's job to keep him fed. So she did.

Every morning she rose before dawn and ran past the fields. She never killed where she lived. People might get suspicious.

But what about the skeleton in the car? Wasn't that a foreshadowing of Tayna's death?

Nah.

It was just George Krase.

George worked in the same office. He wasn't dead. He was just shy. And he had a crush on Tanya. So he dressed up in weird costumes every day, hoping to get her attention.
Two days ago, George dressed as a pirate, And the day before that, a mermaid.

George wasn't exactly Tanya's type. For one, he was alive.
But maybe, just maybe, someday…

August 9

Dear Maggie

A summons.

Humming, I grab my gauntlets.

So many atrocities at the festival.

I melt…

August 10

Dear Maggie,

The favor's most proper.

But a dishonest weapon disrupts the trend.

A hypnotic comet streaks the sky

I scoop and scoop, but the fluid pours out and won't go back.

August 11
Dear Maggie

The bluntness of the ambush enraged this daughter.

Tie the poisonous knot.

Kissing is no more.

With downward hesitation the guillotine sinks into brush.

Common prayers don't work over there.

Murderer, you are.

August 12
Dear Maggie,

I'm a nervous wreck. My head is pounding; my stomach is churning. I'm not sleeping well, and I'm not staying awake very well, either.

Aunt Silly and I haven't washed dishes in a week. So I decided to wash all of them.

I had just picked up a stack of dirty plates to set in the hot soapy water when CRASH!

They slipped from my hands and sprayed glass bits from end of the kitchen floor to the another.

Maggie, I actually burst into tears!

Aunt Silly was nice, though. She stopped twisting wire and helped me clean up the mess.

Then we did the dishes together, me washing and her drying.

Afterwards, I helped her twist wire. We smoked and talked, but we did not laugh so much.

Maggie, I'm so uneasy.

August 13
Dear Maggie,

I think Dad sees how this is affecting me.

In fact, when our eyes met on the porch tonight, he looked very concerned.

Do you think he's forgiven me?

August 14
Dear Maggie,

I can't write.

I can't sleep.

I can't concentrate.

Maybe I should just quit. What's the point in finishing the world's greatest werewolf story when I've already failed Dad?

Why do I need that fucking weirdo in the basement anyway? Why won't the story come without him?

WHY????

August 15

Dear Maggie,

Dad came into my room last night just as I was falling asleep.

He's been working late a lot.

He sat on the edge of the bed and said, "I'm sorry, Mouse."

And I said, "I'm sorry, too, Dad."

No one said anything. Then I said, "Dad, I wasn't trying to snoop. You were sick, and Aunt Silly said you had a vet emergency, and then I..."

Dad sighed and said, "I know, Mouse."

"I thought maybe something bad happened."

Dad sighed again and said nothing.

After a long, long while, Dad asked, "How is the werewolf story coming?"

"Slow," I admitted. "Slow, but it's coming."

"Is it still a love story?" Dad asked.

"Of course."

Dad didn't answer. Maggie, I think I fell asleep because the next thing I knew, Dad was brushing the back of my hand and saying, "Good night, don't let the werewolves bite."

My eyes flew open, but the room was empty.

Maybe I dreamed it?

Anyway, I am free.

First stop: Gordan James' house.

August 15
Dear Maggie,

Now that my prison term is up, it's time to check on the "other" prisoner.

I'm hoping to sneak over later today.

Aunt Silly is behind on orders and needs my help.

Soon, Maggie, I swear it. Soon.

August 16

Dear Maggie

I saw him today, Maggie. I finally saw the wolf boy today.

My heart is partly breaking, partly puzzled.

Everything is the same. But everything feels different.

The wolf boy is still in the basement.

He's still chained to a spike in the concrete by leg cuffs.

He's still hairy and dirty.

He's still naked. (Oh, Maggie...)

The floor is still covered in shit and flies.

No beast or person (well, maybe a few persons) should be treated like this. Especially a wolf boy who's inspired the greatest werewolf love story ever written!

But he still looks well-fed, rested, and not in pain, and he still doesn't look scared. I'm sooo glad because I need him to stay fine until I finish the book.

So everything is the same. Except...

He doesn't look puzzled when she sees me. In fact, I'm pretty sure he recognizes me, knows me. I don't even need to pound on the bubble glass anymore. Today he was sitting on his haunches and looking toward the window, almost as if he was expecting me.

And he seems more...confident. Maggie, how can that be?

How can everything be exactly the same for a prisoner, a prisoner, Maggie, a prisoner; I'm certain he's a prisoner; how can everything be exactly the same for a prisoner, EXCEPT his mindset, his spirit?

Unless it's me. Could that be it, Maggie?

Could I be seeing this boy differently as the story develops? Am I the one that's changing while he stays the same?

I don't know how long I crouched at the window, but when I "came to," the sun was waning, and the wolf boy had fallen asleep.

I scrambled to my feet and hurried home as fast as I could, chapter eight singing in my head.

August 16
Dear Maggie,

Aunt Silly had dinner almost ready when I arrived.

"Look, Caryn." She pointed to the fry pan at the back of the stove. "Thinly sliced."

"They look great," I said as I hurried to my room.

"The story?" she called.

"Yes!" I called back. "Long walks help the muse!"

Maggie, you wouldn't believe how fast I started typing out chapter eight!

August 17
Dear Maggie,

I worked on chapter eight far into the night and overslept this morning. It's not quite done, but I can share my progress so far.

Aunt Silly was grinning at me when I finally plodded to the kitchen for food. My throat felt all scratchy, and my muscles felt stiff and sore.

I ran the tap to get the water nice and cold and grabbed an apple from her fruit bowl on the counter. I sipped the water to soothe my scratchy throat, and then I bit into a crunchy apple.

How can muscles ache from staying up late? Is this how "Carrynne" feels after a night of hunting on the hill?

As I threw my core away, the phone rang. Aunt Silly answered it, and her face scrunched up at the voice, and she kept casting glances in my direction.

Fuck you, I thought.

I left the kitchen, shut the bathroom door, and then tiptoed back into the hall just in time to hear Aunt Silly ask, "All of it, Fred?"

Dad said something I obviously couldn't hear. And then she said, "Did you report it?"

I stifled an exasperated sigh. Dumb fucking tourists! I can't tell you how many times Dad's had to report neglect and abuse of their "pets."

I swear, Maggie, half the people in the world, maybe more, aren't fit to own a dust bunny!

Anyway, here is about half of chapter eight. Isn't it great? So you like how I superimposed my grounding frustration into Carrynne.

"They" say, "Write what you know."

Right?

Write?

Chapter 8:
"Turning Point"

Waking up on the kitchen floor is not so bad these days. I'm still

covered in enough fat that the hard
surface is not too cold, even with the
air conditioning running. And because
every night is now a full moon night
because Peter Stumpp, my clock friend
from The Clock Man, keeps Randy time,
my muscles are well-defined and hard.
Nothing aches, except my heart when I
am away from Randy.

I rise and head to the bathroom
for a shower, watching the rippling
through my sleek skin as I move. Such
beautiful coordination, so necessary
for a successful hunt.

I turn the handle to hot and the
spray fills the room with steam. After
grabbing a pink wash rag off the
shelf, I step into the tub, slide my
mother's old pink plastic curtain
across the rod to keep the water off
the floor, and pick up the pink soap
from its soap-caked tray.

The hot water beads over the fat
and turns it pink. I lather up the
wash rag and scrub through the fat,
scraping off dried blood and bits of
flesh from last night's kill along
with sweat and dirt and grease. Then I
unscrew the cap from the bottle of
golden baby shampoo and lather up my
matted hair. I'm taking a journey
tonight, and I can't look like a wild
animal.

When the water finally streams
across my skin and runs clear down the
drain, and when the room smells as
clean as the kitchen when the laundry

comes off the line and into the house,
I silence the water and squeeze the
droplets out of my hair. I step onto
the soft shag of the pink rug and grab
a pink towel from the shelf. Once all
the water is blotted, I knot the towel
around my waist and reset Peter
Stumpp.

Tonight cannot be a full moon.
Tonight I will locate and destroy the
aconite that is hurting my Randy. And
then I will find my father's
rebellious rowan cane. So today I
rest.

I fling myself onto my bed, face
up, and stare at the ceiling. The room
is too bright for me, even in the
waning afternoon light, making me glad
I've become so nocturnal.
But tonight will be a very busy night.
I grope beneath my pillow for the key
and smile when I touch its sleek metal
and jagged shape.

I close my eyes to rest.

When I open them again, I'm on a
wide path in an endless forest, with
bracken and trees a blackish pine
green and new moon in a sky the color
of ebony. The path stretches behind
me, and it beckons in front of me, so
I know the way is right for me.

I'm wearing my long white
nightgown; my feet are bare and
touching the earth. I'm seeking,
seeking. I'm still the huntress, but
my prey is knowledge, the whereabouts
of the aconite. To ask its mistress to

give up her secrets, I must approach the mistress directly. I never dared before tonight. Pretense always works well for me, but it won't do now.

Although the breeze is still, the night air cools my still-damp hair. The woods are silent, and no cheeky creatures break that spell. Yet I know whispering shadows lurk just out of sight and sound, and that my approach isn't going unnoticed.

I see her now, just ahead, standing at the crossroads with her back to me. She is wearing the same white gown, and the same copper hair flows behind it. A baying dog guards each entrance of this triple-road passage, the place where my past, present, and future intersects. The baying rings in my ears and my heart pounds excitedly.

I lift one foot and put it down. I lift the other and put it down, too. I feel the dull ache of pebbles, long embedded into the hardpacked dirt; I feel the sharp pricks of straying pine needles and shards of soda pop bottles; my feet are coated with powdered dirt. Step after step, my feet lead me until I'm close enough to smell her pink soap and golden baby shampoo, and I prostrate before her in the dust.

In my heart, I make known my request, and it smells like patchouli as it wafts up to her.

Suddenly, I'm at the edge of the woods wearing three gardening gloves on each hand. Each glove is baby pink with a green cuff.
It's the hour before dawn, so I must work quickly.

It's the hour before light, but I don't need light to see the work I'm about to undertake.

For my eyes glow with a green phosphorescence. And I see my prey as if I had the light of day.

With their teeny white eyes, they stare at me, defiantly,from their blueish purple hoods.

They stand firm on their sickly yellow-green stalks, silently daring me. They're full of deadly poison from petals to roots, which must be curling tightly into the ground.

I laugh out loud, a battle cry. It resounds throughout the quiet night into millions of clinking echoes.

I raise my hands, gallows in gardening gloves, and snicker.

With my head back and snout to the moon, I roar long and loudly.

I lunge into their ranks. To and fro, back and forth, pulling, ripping, tearing, shredding. Like a crazed starving she-beast let loose from her cage, I ravage their numbers until the enemy is destroyed, and Randy is avenged.

I throw the gloves into the grove and plop to the ground, legs splayed, panting. After a long, long,

long time, I realize I'm lying on my
back on the bed, looking up at the
ceiling, and panting very hard and
fast. The towel has fallen to the
floor, and I'm shivering from the air
conditioning.

It's already late afternoon, but
the sun is still too bright for a
nocturnal creature like me. My stomach
growls for raw food; I feel weak and
faint with hunger and with a hunger
for Randy.

August 18

Dear Maggie,

Let me tell you about this bitch I met today.

At Dad's office, of all places.

She's old and fat and stinks of last week's trash. She doesn't smile, and even the kittens growled at her.

Her name is Ruthie...something.

Something so stupid I don't remember it.

But she's going to run the office side of Dad's practice.

"Dad, where in the fuck did you find her?"

But Dad is still mad at me for trespassing and isn't very talkative. All he said is, "I need someone I can trust to handle clerical duties for me."

Ouch!

I hang around a bit. She does seem very efficient. In thirty minutes, she had the backlog of filing and billing done. She had restocked the supply room, noted what we needed, and placed an order by phone.

I still didn't like her.

"Dad," I asked again right before lunch. "If she's so great, why did she need a job here in SHELBY?"

He sighed, in an exasperated and not very happy with me way. Is he going to stay mad at me forever?

"Because," he said, drawing out the word. "Her last employer cut her pay. So she quit."

"Well, you do take in stray dogs," I quipped.

Nope, Dad wasn't going to bite. And he sure as hell wasn't going to fire her.

She is definitely not Wendy, that's for sure.

So I wrote a werewolf story about her. I made her this disgruntled office worker who got a pay cut for being, well disgruntled. Here's the story:

One night during a full moon, Ruthie Something stays and works very late. Why? I don't know. Maybe because she's too disgruntled to go home.

Yes, that's it. She's too disgruntled to go home and cook dinner for her lazy-ass husband Joe who drinks all day and throws his beer cans on the floor.

So she stays late. But she has to leave sometime. And when she does, she locks the door behind her and glances up.

The moon is full and ripe. A dark cloud glides across the sky and partially blocks the moon.
Ruthie shivers and hugs herself. She likes to read weird, horror stories. And she suddenly remembers the weird one she read last night, about a werewolf that only eats disgruntled office workers.

She hears a howl in the distance.

So she starts to run. She's able to run because she doesn't wear high heels. She wears the type of shoes my

Grandma used to wear, a little high in the ankles and with laces she ties in double knots.

As she runs, the howl keeps pace. And get closer.

So Ruthie runs faster. And the howls get louder and near her ear.

As you might guess, Ruthie never made it home that night. And her husband Joe would have starved to death, except...

The next month during a full moon, Joe heard a howl outside his window. A very familiar sounding howl.

And then next thing he heard was, "Damn it! I told you to pick up those beer cans! And now you're going to pay!"

I know, Maggie, I know. Taking my bows (not bow wows).

August 18
Dear Maggie,

Restless like a werewolf...

Can't sleep. Can't write.

I really need to go back to Gordan James house.

August 19
Dear Maggie

August 25th is almost here.

It's almost here, Maggie!!!!!! And I'm not done!

FUCK!

August 20

Dear Maggie.

Something terrible happened today at Dad's office.

He was in his actual office catching up on paperwork when he called me to bring Tabitha's chart. That's the tabby that died of cancer, remember?

I wondered why he needed the chart. But these days, I'm not comfortable questioning Dad.

The trust between us is strained like an overstretched rubber band. And I don't know if it will ever snap back.

But as I handed Dad Tabitha's chart, my eyes traveled to the window, and my heart nearly stopped.

All the aconite plants were gone.

"Dad?" I asked, my mind racing to catch up to my disbelieving eyes. "Where are they?"

I didn't have to specify. He knew.

He flipped a page and kept writing.

"Gone," he said in a distracted way.

"Gone? What the fuck do you mean, 'gone?'"

Dad closed the chart and handed it back to me.

"They're gone, Mouse," Dad said in a very flat and toneless voice. "Someone ripped them out."

Maggie, I'm so confused. Who would rip out all the aconite?
And then I had a frightening thought.
Could I have sleepwalked to Dad's office and ripped out all the aconite?
And why would I do that when Dad needs it to calm anxious animals?
Maggie, what in the actual fuck is going on?

August 20
Dear Maggie,

307

So I explored.

I waited until Dad went into surgery, and I went back to where he used to grow the aconite.

Someone had ripped it up all right.

The ground looked as if giant moles had razed it. Not dead plant was in sight. Dad must have cleaned up the aconite corpses.

I walked up and down the area, but I wasn't being random.

I was stalling. I knew the grove of trees where "Carrynne" threw the gloves.

Finally, Maggie, I shoved the branches aside.

And there lay the same old pink gardening gloves I'd described in my story, right down to the green cuffs.

And I saw something else. Something horrible and scary.

Something that made me scream for a very long time. Even after Dad came out and saw it and threw up on the spot.

Even after he yelled and yelled for Ruthie to call the police.

Even after the neighbors gathered around us, pushing, trying to see, too.

Even after the police and Aunt Silly showed up, and Aunt Silly held me tightly and smoothed my hair and murmured into my ear. Even then, Maggie, I could not stop screaming.

I screamed half the night, even after Aunt Silly drove me home and plopped me on the couch and wrapped me in blankets and plied me with hot tea in a chipped pink mug.

Because next to the gardening gloves, poking out of the ground, was a hand covered in colonies of maggots.

On the index finger was one of Aunt Silly's moonstone rings.

The ring and the finger belonged to someone nice who would never be a bride in September.

Wendy.

August 21

Dear Maggie,

Aunt Silly is so wonderful for a human!

She camped at my bedroom door last night.

I was sitting on the couch sipping tea when she got up to pee. She was gone a long, long while. You'd think she was the one drinking all the tea.

Then I heard a scuffing and a bunch of grunts. Next thing I see is Aunt Silly dragging her mattress toward my room.

I did smile...I didn't have it in me to laugh. I set my chipped pink mug on the coffee table and stumbled down the hall to help.

"Auntie, what in the fuck are you doing?" I demanded.

"What the hell does it look like?" she retorted. "You had one helluva scare, and I'm keeping the heeby jeebies away from you tonight!"

So I helped her drag the mattress near my door. The room's too small for the mattress to actually fit in the room.

And that's where she slept all night.

Dad actually had to step over her to reach the bathroom.

August 21
Dear Maggie,

The terror of the missing aconite and Wendy's demise is still hanging around me like a fading demon this morning. The terror is real, but waning, thanks to the August morning sunshine.

Still...

Wendy was a genuinely good person. She was kind to animals and good to Dad. Who would want to hurt her? It's so unfair!!!

Thinking about her was unthinkable. I. Just. Can't.

So I thought about my looming deadline instead. So I wrote (and rewrote and rewrote) the last part of chapter eight.

My inner spirit feels like the legend of the two wolves...or maybe I should say "two werewolves."

One is fighting for a tragic outcome; the other is fighting for true love to triumph. I want the triumph, of course, but a force inside of me that feels apart from me wants the tragedy.

You can see struggle in the rest of this chapter, Maggie...as well as shades of my trauma from Wendy's murder.

I guess I'm still writing what I know.

With that, I give you (drum roll) the rest of chapter eight.

Quickly I prepare the flying ointment; even more quickly I glide through the air to my wolf mate. I slip through the chink and scream long and hard and strong. I scream again and again; I never want to stop screaming.

Randy is huddled in the corner, beaten, lacerated, and bloody. His matted fur sticks to the open wounds like a twisted kindergarten art project. One side of his face is swollen blue, except for the black eye swollen shut.

Randy! Who did this to you?

His mind forms the words with great difficulty, and I can see each syllable causes his brain excruciating pain.

My father. He went to get aconite and found it ripped it out the ground. He was so angry, Carrynne. He stormed in here and beat me with his stick of mountain ash.

I will help you, Randy. I will help you now!

Suddenly, I'm in front of Randy. I get down on all fours.

Get on my back, Randy, I will help you.

But Randy doesn't have the strength to climb up. He's famished and maimed, and the fading sunlight further saps his vitality; only moonlight restores it. And I, the female, am not strong enough to pick him up. I crouch and cry while my beaten beast boy tries to comfort me with a weak paw.

Suddenly, I know what to do.

Wait here, Randy. I will be right back.

I float out of the chink, over the hill, and to the meadow where the unicorns prance and graze. The terrain was mottled with plants unicorns eat. I can't make out each herbaceous magical food, but I know what they are. There's mandrake, low to the ground with its wide ovate leaves and tiny dusky flowers; There's henbane with its sticky hairy, gray-green leaves and sickly yellow flowers with an evil muddy eye in their centers. There's wormwood with leaves of silvery green and sleepy yellow buds.

The air pounds with hundreds of grinding teeth as the great-horned beasts decimate every living green being with their unholy appetites.

Unicorns charge, especially when someone disturbs their eating or mating. She who hesitates will surely be pulverized. But a unicorn is helpless to defend itself when the attacker approaches without its body, and mine is unconscious on my bed at home.

They sense me. The chewing stops; the lift their heads; their eyes dart nervously over the expanse. I kill one with a single blow and drag it by its horn all the way back to Randy, laying it at his feet.

I brought food. Then you won't be so weak to climb onto my back.

Randy instantly tears through its tough hide and devours its tender flesh, unicorn blood oozing into his scraggly facial hair. He saves two of the legs for me, smiling cunningly as he nudges them my way with his foot.

For you, Carrynne. So you have the strength to help me.

Ravenously I devour them, skin, meat, and bones. Just three bites each and not a scrap was left.

Then once more, I crouch on my hands and knees, my virtual nose pointing toward the chink. It takes a long time for Randy to climb up, but he finally does, entwining his fingers and legs around mine. Soon I'm flying through the sky, stretched out like Daedalus in the August twilight. With a cool wind tickling my ears, I carry my wolf mate to my suburban lair. I soar between a fiery sunset and graying fields, while a poem forms in my mind.

Come fly with me through a summer night, where darkness reigns over the plains, and light takes flight from a sky as red as blood...

From above me I hear, *Thank you, Carrynne.*

I will not let more bad things happen to you Randy.

You can't prevent it, Carrynne. My father is very, very powerful.

Is he more powerful than a werewolf, Randy?

I hear a soft, sinister chuckle.

Of course not, Carynne. That's why he beats me with mountain ash and immobilizes me with aconite.

Well, he cannot immobilize you with aconite any longer, Randy, because the aconite is all gone.

But I am still trapped in this house, Carrynne. As long as I remain his prisoner, he will beat me with his mountain ash stick. And he can grow more aconite and immobilize me again.

Fear ripples through me, but I squelch it. If I start to shake, I might drop Randy. Then he'd be worse off than he is now. He'd no longer be beaten prisoner in a lonely basement. He'd be smashed and dead.

Don't think horrible words, Randy. I will free you. I will find a way. I promise.

August 21

Dear Maggie,

Who is the actual fuck ripped out all Dad's aconite?

Who killed Wendy?

August 22

Dear Maggie,

Chapter nine is just not coming.

And my werewolf love story keeps veering in its own direction. Does this happen to all writers?

I've tried so hard to protect Carrynne's and Randy's love; I really, really have. But no matter how I try, different words wind up on the page.

I feel like, the more I go to visit the wolf boy, the more I lose control of the story.

And yet, when I don't see him, the words don't flow.

Now, and this is going to sound far out, but...

Do you think the wolf boy is a hypnotist? DI know he's "helping" me write my story but...

So you think he's actually writing my story, at least parts of it?

Think about it, Maggie, before you answer.

Remember how much I struggled to write it before I found him? And whenever I get stuck, seeing him "unsticks" the stuck ideas.

Well, if it's true, he's NOT getting co-author status! And he's NOT getting any of my royalties, my billions!

But, still, Maggie...

Do you think Gordon James is keeping him in the basement because he's dangerous, that maybe he hypnotizes people to do things that are bad or against their will – like ripping our Dad's aconite and murdering Wendy?

That's pretty far-fetched, though. Don't you think, Maggie?

Maybe the debaucher who ripped out the aconite only dug a hole to bury the plants. Maybe Wendy stumbled upon the foul deed, and the aconite ripper had no choice but to...

Or maybe the deed was already done, and she just happened to fall through the soft earth. Maybe she hit her head and died. Or maybe she suffocated.

I think I'm going to try sneaking out of the house tonight to you know where.

Yes, Maggie, I know it's risky. Yes, Maggie, I know Gordon James might catch me.

But my story has taken a twisty turn that, I hate to say it, is unsettling me.

I'm glad I only have one chapter left.

And before I write it, I'm going to look that wolf-boy in the eye and remind him who's story it is!

August 23

Dear Maggie,

You were right. Sneaking out of the house at night is too risky. I didn't do it.

However, I did see the wolf boy for a little bit yesterday. But the details are blurred.

I remember finishing some orders with Aunt Silly in the morning and then heading to Dad's office after lunch to help him in the afternoon.

But before I went to Dad's, I cut over to Fifth Street "for just a few minutes." The rest is fuzzy.

Even after I finally made it to Dad's later in the afternoon, I felt as if I was walking in that space between alert and asleep. You know the feeling, Maggie...when you wake up, but you can't quite wake up.

It was like that.

And then last night, I had a very strange and scary dream.

I dreamt I went to a box shoppe with Aunt Silly. Yes, you heard me. A box shoppe, a shoppe that sells every size and shape of box you can imagine.

In the dream, Aunt Silly is taking a long time to talk "shoppe" with the shoppe owner. He's very tall, about nine feet tall, with enormous muscles. He's got long, thick, white, curly hair and a matching beard. His name is Mr. Zeus.

I get bored and wander through the shoppe looking at all the boxes. I wander for miles, it seems, and soon I come to a vast garden with a trickling stream running right through the middle. On each side of the garden are walls of shelves. They go higher than the clouds, run on forever, and they are full of boxes.

I keep walking and dusk settles, turning the landscape a misty, darkening periwinkle. I hear the whining of a puppy, and I call, "Puppy! Puppy! Where are you, little puppy?"

After walking and walking some more, the sound settles into the farthest right corner. I skip over the stones in the bubbling stream, and when I reach the corner, I realize the garden is a giant tent.

So I pull the flap aside. The puppy's cries are coming from inside a silver box. The box is sitting on a rotting tree trunk in a field of scratchy thick grasses, daisies, black-eyed Susans, clover, and Queen Anne's Lace. The field is bordered with wild roses, and the air smells pungent with their combined perfumes.

The silver box is studded with moonstones and a green phosphorescence is wafting from the cracks where the lid meets the rest of the box.

Next to the box is a silver key full of hecatolite stones.

As I put my hands on each side of the box, a voice calls out from the inside of the box, "Let me out, Caryn! Let me out, let me out! Let me out! Open the box and let me out!"

I'm very intrigued. I pick up the key, unlock the box, and peer inside.

I see a little white wolfish puppy holding its little pointed face between its paws and crying.

"Puppy" I asked.

The puppy lowered its paws and calmly gazed at me with eyes of green phosphorescence.

"Puppy?" I ask. "Puppy, are you OK?"

The puppy leaps out of the box and dark clouds of chirring insects flutter after him. They disperse into the sky until all the world is terrifyingly dark.

The box grows and grows until it's about half the size of me. I grip the edges with both hands and look inside. But I only see darkness, a swirling, everlasting, black hole of nothing.

"Caryn," a low voice chuckles. "Oh, Caryn..."

I whirl around. The puppy's gone. Standing behind me is Gordan James' hairy wolf boy. He's naked, full of flies, and smells like shit.

And he's smirking at me with all the cockiness a wolf boy can muster.

Which is a lot.

I woke up with a headache and my heart pounding.

With my eyes barely open and without even stopping to pee, I trudged to my desk chair, rolled up a sheet of paper, and rapidly plucked out letters.

This chapter reads like a twisty vine. Every time it curved another way, I brought it back to where I wanted it to go.

So far, Carrynne and Randy's love is protected.

So far...

Chapter 9:
"Finally Free"

Night has fully blossomed by the time our feet touch down by my back door, and the wild roses that grow up around my house wrap us in its spicy aura. The sky is drenched in darkness, and all nature feels it. The stars aren't whispering their faraway secrets; the katydids and crickets have silenced their songs; and even yard toads have stifled their shrill calls.

This is what happens when you bring a werewolf to your home on a summer evening. I turn to Randy to see if he feels it, too, and I meet the moon's glow in his eyes.

We pass through the door and glide to the bathroom. He looked at me, and I looked at him.

His hair was scraggly and long and dirty and matted, even the hair on his ears.

So I took out my brush and very gently started brushing out his matted fur, starting with his legs and working my way up. Randy winced, but he did not cry out, even though I knew each stroke smarted.

But I took my time. I rested my hand along the hairline and slowly eased the brush through each tangle.

All the way up his legs. All the way down his arms.

He did not squirm or try to run away.

His back.

His chest.

And his glowing eyes followed every stroke.

I brushed out the hair on top of his head.

And the hair on his face.

Then I filled the deep tub with hot water. He climbed in and lowered himself far into the water, and the water swam around his neck.

I grabbed the baby shampoo and lathered him up, starting with his feet, his claws, and working my way up his legs. His wounds turn the suds and water a frothy pink

I lathered up his hands and up his arms.

His back.

His chest.

His face.

Several times, I lifted the plug to let the bloody water drain out. Several times, I turned the tap back on and refilled the tub with plenty of steaming water to sooth away the rawness of his open wounds and cleanse away the blood and grime.

I lathered up the hair on his head.

But I didn't just suds him up and rinse him with the bath water using pink plastic cup by the sink. I gave him a nice massage, too, starting at the top of his head and working my way to the base of his tail.

I felt all his muscles relax as my hands and tips of my fingers gently kneaded his muscles. Then I rinsed away the suds, the dirt, and the last of his trepidations. He was actually smiling by the time I started rubbing him dry with a pink fluffy towel.

"Good Randy," I told him in my real voice, over and over in my most soothing tone. "Good Randy."

When his fur is nearly dry, I throw the towel on the floor.

Follow me, Randy.

He follows me to my bedroom. I pick up a clean brush from the top of my dresser, sit on my bed, and pat the spot next to me.

He sits on my bed, and I brush out his clean and snarled fur once more. Again I start at his feet and work my way up with the greatest of tenderness. Fur snaps easily when wet.

When every piece of fur lays flat and dry, he stretches out across my bed, and he grins a satisfied grin. I can see he's enjoying how the mattress yields to his form, a feat impossible for basement concrete. I lie beside him and sense his breathing. No need to hunt tonight.

Unicorn meat is magical meat. One unicorn equals twelve people. We won't be hungry until tomorrow night. Tonight, we can just be. Tonight, we can just…

What's this, Carrynne?

He pulls my silver hecatolited key out from under my pillow. I scowl and swipe at it.

It's the key to my house, Randy. Give it back!

He holds it up close, the better to see my dear key, and the hecatolite sparkles in his moonlight.

So it was you, Carrynne. You held the key the whole time.

I yank at his hair. *Give me my key!*

He turns to me with gleaming green eyes. *That's why you killed and ate your parents, Carrynne?*

Yes. I wanted the key, and they would not give me the key.

Why did you want this key, Carrynne?

He sounds annoyed. Well, I am even more annoyed.

Because I thought it was pretty, and I wanted it. It's my key now, so you'd better give it to me.

I've waited so long for you to let me out, Carrynne.

Let you out?

Randy moves close to my face and jabs me with the key.

Let me out, Carrynne! Let me out, let me out! Let me out! Open the box and let me out!

My mind crashes like a stack of dropped plates. In splinters and shards, the memories return until they're blinding and blistering, like staring into a noon sun in July.

When I was a little girl, I had a grandmother who lived in the woods. She wasn't really my grandmother, but she was old and weird and lived alone in the middle of a field, and she grew herbs that my mother took to Rosie to sell and then brought the money back to Grandmother's house.

The house always reminded me of a gingerbread house. It was painted cookie crumb brown with a roof as sweet as sugar cakes, and sugar plum shutters and trim. My mother and I always visited on Monday to give Grandmother her money and to gather more herbs for Rosie.

I remember Grandmother never ate vegetables or fruit or grain. She only ate meat, and she wasn't tidy about it, either. Her floors and grass were littered with bones. And she always wore black.

But Grandmother was especially kind to children. She liked to leave out sweet treats for them to eat as they passed by her house. This wasn't just a single plate of Toll House Inn cookies, although she left those, too, and they never melted, no matter how high the sun rose in the sky or how scorching it sent down its rays.

No, she laid out rich slices of layered chiffon cake drizzled with chocolate, wedges of rhubarb pie and banana cream pie, cubes of colored gelatin, ice cream snowballs with strawberry sauce, pudding topped with maraschino cherries, pineapple upside down cake, squares of carrot cake with cream cheese frosting, and lots of cookies: peanut butter, sugar, shortbread, oatmeal, and fruit bars.

As I said, everything stayed fresh and nothing ever grew sludgy.

Still, my mother never let me go to Grandmother's house alone. And she never let me eat anything Grandmother baked.

And you wonder why I killed my mother?

On the very last Monday that we visited Grandmother, my mother knocked and knocked, but Grandmother did not answer. So my mother finally took out the hecatolite key, unlocked the door, and went inside the dim, dank house, with me trailing behind her.

The house reeked of raw hamburger, more than usual. We called, "Grandmother" as we traipsed through the house, but no one answered. Finally we had just one room to check: the bedroom. I hoped Grandmother was sick in bed. When she was, we played our favorite game.

"Oh, grandmother, what big ears you have!"

"All the better to hear you with."

"Oh, grandmother, what big eyes you have!"

"All the better to see you with."

"Oh, grandmother, what big hands you have!"

"All the better to grab you with!"

"Oh, grandmother, what a horribly big mouth you have!"

"All the better to eat you with!"

And then I would pretend to shiver while she licked her lips. At which point, I tossed a raw chicken into her lap.

But Grandmother was not sick in bed. She was dead in bed, eyes staring through me, mouth gaping as if she wanted to speak, and the words had frozen on their way out. Only a silver bullet could leave a pristine hole through a heart like the hole blown through the top of her dress.

My mother hustled me outside, and then I heard her dial my father for help. So I plopped onto an old tree trunk amidst all the sun-bleached bones and sulked. After a while, I heard whimpering.

This was not the sound of human whimpering, but a lonesome, heartrending whimpering, the sound a puppy makes when it's lost its mother. I eased off the stump and wandered around the yard, stepping over remains, peering through brush.

I finally found the puppy, a tan little wolfish cub, hiding behind a fat green shrub and holding its little pointed face between its paws as it cried.

"Puppy" I asked.

The puppy lowered its paws and calmly gazed at me with eyes of green phosphorescence. I reached out to stroke its fur; the puppy clamped its jaws onto my hand.

I screamed long and hard, enough to wake the dead, except none of the dead strewn over the grass actually did wake up. My last memory of that Monday is the sight of my mother running out of the house.

We never went to Grandmother's house again. And whenever we left our own house, we all left together, and my parents locked the doors with the pretty key. My dad developed a limp that summer and walked with a cane.

The rowan cane.

I saw the fear in their eyes when I eyed raw meat with suppressed hunger and howled at the moon with my doleful refrains.

I saw their panic when I restlessly paced the house. No matter how much the moon begged for me, no matter how much I pled for it to rescue me, my parents would not unbolt the doors or unscrew the windows or untie me from the bed post.

With each full moon, my craving grew stronger, unbearable. Only now do I realize the glow of the moon was the glow in Randy's eyes, and my craving for meat and my craving for Randy was the same.

I am a werewolf's mate. *I am a werewolf's mate!*

So I killed them, ground them up with the meat grinder they used to make sausage for church suppers, and ate them to draw me closer to Randy. And now I owned the key, and no one could take it away from me, not even Randy. And now I knew why.

I push Randy to the door.

Go, Randy, hurry. Hurry back to your spirit. I am coming to save you with my key!

He understands and wanes, quite slowly. He fades to translucent and then dims to an outline. The last of Randy to leave are his eyes, and they glow with deep phosphorescence for a full minute after the rest of him vanishes.

I pull my long white nightgown over my head and grab my moonstone. If I am to take the real key and free the real Randy's body, I have to take the real me, in my body, to his real prison at the bottom of Grandmother's old house. Flying by magic ointment will not work tonight. I must walk to Grandmother's old house in the dark, with the moonstone to guide my way. A simple spirit, no matter how real, could not take the real key.

Poor, poor, poor little wolf boy, I think as I lock the door and pocket my key, a key full of pride and purpose.

And then suddenly I'm at the house. I'm standing at the back, where two sets of wolf tracks lead away from the house. It's the same side where Grandmother had a door. But the door is gone.

Or is it?

And I remember…

Randy, you can get out?

Of course. And you can get in.

I can't see the chink because I'm not in my wolf spirit. But the key knows the way. I sweep it over the wall as I slowly move along the house. Finally, an outline of the door emerges. I quickly slip the key inside the lock and open the door!

"Randy!" I yell in my real voice. "Randy! I've come to free you!"

I hear whining from the basement, like a dog in pain. I run down the stairs and see Randy, just like I saw him on the very first day, except his hand is not infected.

He's chained to the wall, and his raggedy clothes are nearly threadbare. His straight brown hair still hangs past his shoulders and smells like golden baby shampoo, and his facial hair is still baby fine, scraggly, and even longer than last time.

He's not sleeping. He's sitting on his haunches, as if he's expecting me. His bruises are gone, and his wounds are healed. He smells of pink soap.

I rush across the room and drop to my knees. I insert my key inside the padlock and turn it; the mechanism clicks. I help Randy shed his chains, and then I grab his paw.

"Let's go, Randy," I whisper. "You are free. We are free, We will be together forever."

He looks at me with cunning eyes of emerald green, eyes glittering with carnality so raw I start to drip and shake. They enchant me; he enchants me; and although Randy's chains are scattered across the floor, he's only just begun to bind me to his will, to his spirit, and I am so, so ready to spring into the unknown with my werewolf mate and dwell in murkiness and mayhem forever.

We sprint up the stairs, and then we dash out the door, where we stop short.

Because there stands Mr. McCallister, looking as young as his missing person pictures. He's wearing a three-piece suit, a bowler hat, and a watch and chain. He has a receding hairline and clipped mustache.

And he's gripping a gleaming silver rifle in one hand and my long-lost rowan cane in the other.

August 24

Oh my God, Maggie!

Oh my God! Oh my God! Oh, my God!

The most terrible thing has happened. Please be quiet and let me get it out.

Oh. My. God...

OK, let me think.

OK.

Like I told you, I planned to see Gordan James' wolf boy prisoner before I wrote chapter ten. But I couldn't go right away.

Aunt Silly needed my help with deliveries. And then Ruthie went home sick, and I helped Dad most of the afternoon and into the evening. The tourists kept coming with dumb shit, and Dad performed two emergency surgeries, both time for broken legs, both times because the dogs got hit by cars.

We ordered from Mario's Pizza Pies Supreme. Dad sent me home around twilight.

"I have a lot of paperwork, Mouse," Dad said, sounding very tired and reaching inside his pocket for his dime store glasses.

"I'll stay and help," I offered.

But Dad just shook his head sadly and said, "You can't help with this."

I knew that.

As I started for the door, he said, "Caryn."

I turned around. He was smiling, a weak and exhausted smile. And he said, "If you really want to help, finish your novel. Your birthday is in two days. You need to type 'THE END' before you turn eighteen."

"I know, Dad. I know."

So that's why, even though it was getting dark outside, and Gordan James was either coming home or was probably already home, I did not go straight back to Aunt Silly's.

Instead, I slipped to the supply room and grabbed a flashlight.

I left the office, skirted around to Fifth Street and plunged through the hedge.

It was the first time I'd crawled across Gordan James' backyard in the dark. I could make out the outline of the house. Not a single light was on. But now was not the time for the flashlight, not yet I prayed the bubble glass reflected light very badly. I prayed hedges were thick enough to block any reflected light.

I did not need light to find the wolf boy's window, not anymore. I crawled right up to it and crouched near the glass, waiting. The only sound was the thud-thud-thud-thud of my heart in my ears.

I was safe.

I snapped on the light, stifled a scream, and snapped the light back off. I rocked back and forth on my heels to calm myself. The inside of my head exploded into one giant

NOOOOOOOOOOOOOOOOOOOOOOOOOOOOOOOO OOOOOOOOOOOOOOOOOOOOOOOOOOOOOOOO OOOOOOOOOOOOOOOOOOOOOOOOOOOOOOOO OOOOOOOOOOOOOO!!!!!!!!!!!!!!!!!!!!!!!!!!!!!!!!!!!!!!!

!!!
!!!

And a man yelled, "Hey, you! You, there!"

Maggie, I ran. I ran with all the speed I could force out of my legs, right across Gordan James yard. I ran through the hedge, down the sidewalk, dodging the scant neighborhood traffic, and flagged down a passing police car.

"Help!" I screamed. "Help! Help!"

The car squealed to a stop. Before I could speak, Gordan James' voice yelled, "Arrest her! She tried breaking into my office."

"He's lying!" I screeched. "He's got a teenage boy chained and beaten bloody in his basement. Please save him! PLEASE!"

"You idiot!" Gordan James shouted.

With lights spinning and sirens shrieking, the police car roared away. Gordan James sped after it, on foot.

Not me. I went the other way. I didn't stop running until I reached Dad's office. It was night for real now, and I banged on his door with all my might!

Dad peered out the window and then hastily undid all the bolts. I fell into his arms, screaming and crying.

"Caryn Alaina, what in the world..." Dad began, pulling me away and searching my eyes.

"Dad, I'm a horrible person! I'm so mean, so horrible! I'm horrible, horrible!"

Limping, Dad led me to a chair in the waiting room. He was as white as a kid playing ghost with a sheet and shaking like a leaf in a gale.

"Wait, here. I'll get you're a cup of wat..."

I grabbed his arm. "I killed a boy!"

I thought Dad was going to pass out. He dropped into the chair next to me and clasped my hands. "What boy? Caryn, what happened?"

"Oh, Dad!" I wailed. "It's Gordan James! He's got a naked hairy boy who looks like a wolf chained in his basement! I've known all summer! I spied on Gordan James, followed him home even, and then found the boy. Dad, I'm so sorry! I couldn't help it! But when I saw the boy, I felt like...I felt like I could write...oh, Dad, I'm so mixed up! But I was having such a hard time writing my story...and then when I saw the boy I could...so I kept going back...and going back...every time I ran out of ideas, I went back...I was going to tell; honest I was, cross my heart! But he didn't seem hurt or hungry or scared, and so I thought...oh, Dad, I thought I could wait to tell, you know? I thought I could finish the story and then report Gordan James and then free the boy. But when you told me to go home to finish my story, well, well...I went to Gordan James house to look at the boy. And the boy was beaten SO BADLY! Dad, he looked tomato pulp. He's probably dead, and it's all my...''

Maggie, that's when I noticed something very strange.

Strange and out of place.

Dad's rowan cane was sitting on the reception desk, the rowan cane that used to be mounted on his wall. Why was it not on the wall?

Then I remembered. The full moon.

"The police are there now," I mumbled.

Dad's eyes flickered with alarm. But he stroked my hair and hugged me and told me I did the right thing in coming to him and that everything would be fine.

"But you need to go home, Caryn," Dad said earnestly. "You need to go home and finish that story. I will be there soon."

"Dad, I think Gordan James saw me. What if he's waiting for me? What if he kills me?"

"Gordon James is not waiting for you," Dad said firmly. "He will not kill you. Now go home and write that story."

Just then the door burst open.

It was Gordan James, looking very, very disheveled and frantic.

"Fred, help!" Gordan James cried. "He's gone! My boy is gone!"

Dad hobbled to the desk for the cane.

We all left together.

I headed home.

They did not.

August 24

Dear Maggie,

So I did what Dad told me to do. I wrote chapter ten. To the occasional wail of police sirens and blinding searchlights, I wrote the last chapter.

And I fucking hate it!!!

This is NOT the direction I want my story to go. What is the matter with me???

What is the matter...

Fuck, someone is banging on my door. Gotta run.

But in the meantime...can you please read this and tell me how to get out of it?

Please?

PLEASE???

Because my story cannot end this way!!!

"You!" I cry. "It was you all along!"

Sneering, he raises the rowan cane and holds it over my head. And now I remember! Rowan was mountain ash! My cane kept moving because Mr. McCallister kept stealing it to pummel his son.

"Move out of the way, or I'll beat you down," he threatens. "I'm going to finally kill him."

I stand on tip toes until my powerful eyes meet his mean ones.

"Oh no, you're not!" I yell. "Run, Randy!"

Mr. McCallister knocks me to the ground. I spin around to see Randy tearing across the fields.

I hear the shot ring out and the whizzing of the silver bullet through the air as Randy disappears among the trees.

"Randy!"

Mr. McCallister throws his head back and laughs in a very sinister way. I bite his ankle, and he falls, yelling, "Ouch," and grabbing onto his mangled flesh.

Then I race to the woods
screaming, "Randy!" I scream his name
with each step I take. I'm barreling
down a wide path in an endless forest.
The bracken and trees are a blackish
pine green, and, in the ebony sky, a
golden moon begins to rise. Wild rose
thorns tug at my long white nightgown;
my feet are bare and touching the
earth. I'm still the huntress, but my
prey is knowledge of Randy's safety
and his whereabouts, and my yearnings
smell like patchouli. Pretense always
works well for me, but not tonight.
I'm terrified.

Although the breeze is still,
the night air chills my tears. The
woods are quiet, too quiet, for Randy
does not answer my calls.

I see him now, just ahead,
crumpled at the crossroads. His
silence rings in my ears, and my heart
pounds with mortal fear. With no
regard for the pebbles embedded the
hardpacked dirt, I keep running and
running, over the sharp pricks of pine
needles and shards of soda pop
bottles; my feet slip because they're
powdered with dirt, but still I press
onward until I smell the pink soap,
golden baby shampoo, gunpowder, and
blood.

I can't run anymore, so I drop
to all fours and crawl the rest of the
way, until I reach my Randy and cradle
his hairy body into my lap and murmur

words of comfort as his blood gushes out of the pristine hole in his heart.

I will stay with you, my Randy. You are my past, my present, and my future. I will stay here at the crossroads with you for all eternity. Forever I will wear my white nightgown and keep my feet bare. Forever I will smell like pink soap and golden baby shampoo, here at this place, the intersection of our love, life, and death.

And the only sound I hear forever is the baying of his death howl...

August 24

Dear Maggie

Are you sitting down? Because you are not going to believe what just happened to me.

The knock at the door was Dad and Aunt Silly. At first, I figured I was in trouble until I saw the troubled looks on their faces.

And the potted plant Dad held in his hands.

Aconite. Wolfsbane.

"I suppose you've heard?" I nodded at Aunt Silly.

Dad looked at Aunt Silly.

Aunt Silly lit a cigarette and passed it to me.

Yep, this was serious.

But I played it cool and took a drag. Of course, she had heard. So what? Dad, and Aunt Silly, hated any mistreatment of animals or people who needed help. They'd be on my side, well, except for the part of not speaking up sooner.

Dad sat on the edge of my bed. Aunt Silly settled on the floor.

"Caryn, I should have told you," Dad said.

I took another drag and blew it out like I didn't care. "Told me what?"

"That Gordon James really is. Randolph Monroe McCallister St. Martin the Second. And that I was helping the St. Martins."

Maggie, you know that feeling when you're in an old elevator and it gives a lurch? That's how my stomach felt at his words.

I set the cigarette in the tray and screamed, "You lied to me? You fucking lied to me???"

Dad flinched at each syllable, and then he hung his head.

Aunt Silly reached out and slapped me.

"Watch your tone!" she snapped.

"Prissy, please," Dad said. He used his pleading voice, like the voice Dick used the night he begged to feel me up.

Then Dad looked at me. "Caryn, the St. Martin's son is sick. Very sick. Too sick to be among people. That's why they brought him to me."

My cigarette burned to gray ash. "He was never kidnapped?"

"No," Dad said. "He was born with severe handicaps. One is hypertrichosis, which causes mental retardation and excessive hair growth."

"I figured that out by myself, DAD! So that's an excuse to hide him away? Because his rich, swanky parents are embarrassed?"

"Caryn, it's more than that. The St. Martin's son thinks he's a wolf.''

''So what?''

''After he was born, he bit the nurses in the hospital, enough to draw blood. He bit his parents when they held him, enough to draw blood."

"Dad..."

"A lot of blood."

"You're saying he was born crazy?"

"He even bit..."

Dad sobbed and looked away. I wasn't falling for it. He lied to me. My wonderful, caring Dad lied to me.

"Bit who, Dad?"

Dad shook out his handkerchief and wiped his eyes. "He bit you, Caryn."

"Huh? What? Me?"

Maggie, I admit Dad's words startled me. But only for a minute. It takes a lot to manipulate me.

"What'd he do, Dad? Leap out of his bassinette and bite me?"

"Yes."

"Gimme another cigarette!"

Aunt Silly quickly obliged. Smart lady.

"Or at least, that's what your mom claimed. Remember, your mom and Delores St. Martin were roommates at the hospital.

"Dad, you know Mom's fucking nuts."

"We've tried very hard to protect you, Mouse."

I took a long drag. My alarm clocked ticked very loudly. Dad sounded too old and serious to dismiss.

Goddammit.

"The St. Martins staged the kidnapping and brought their son here. They didn't want to send him to an asylum. They thought I could..."

"Tame him?"

"Yes."

"With aconite?"

That was a long shot. But it was a good shot. Dad just hung his head and whispered, "Yes. For starters."

"It obviously didn't work."

Dad raised his head. "But it does work."

"Bullshit! You've helped a crazy couple keep their crazy kid locked in a basement!"

"And safe."

"You call that safe?"

"We kept everyone safe. Until tonight."

I looked at Aunt Silly. She looked at the floorboards. And Maggie, that's when I heard it, way off in the distance.

It was faint. But it was real.

The howl.

"Safe? There's a scared, sick boy out there who's not safe!"

But my words lacked bite.

"Maybe wounded or dead!"

"He's not wounded," Dad said softly. "He's not dead. And…"

The howl grew louder. Didn't anyone else hear it?

"And what, Dad?"

"And it's not a couple keeping him. Just...Monroe."

"Not Delores?"

The howl was nearly deafening now.

Tears streamed down Dad's cheeks.

"No," he choked out. "She's dead. She was..."

He stopped. The room grew very cold.

"Dad...was she...was she...shot to death?"

He stood up and kissed the top of my head.

"You did it, Caryn," he whispered as he stroked my hair, and his tears made my cheeks wet, too. "You finished your werewolf love story by your birthday. I'm so proud of you."

"Me, too," Aunt Silly sobbed

Dad squeezed my hand. "I love you, Mouse."

They left the room, shutting the door completely shut. Yes, they closed door that never closed all the way.

Bizarre.

The whole scene was bizarre. Why didn't they just tell me the real story from the beginning?

Maggie, suddenly I felt very sorry for them. They seemed so upset and afraid. Even though Dad lied to me, he must've done it for a good reason.

He's my dad and the kindest veterinarian in the whole entire world! I love him!!! And Aunt Silly, she's awesome. I had to reassure them of my love.

Even though they lied to me, they had to know I forgave them.

I leaped up. "Wait!"

Then I heard the click. I ran to the door and tried the knob.

You guessed it, Maggie. Locked.

Stupid. Why would they lock me in the room?

When it's so easy to crawl out of the window.

Dear Maggie,

This might be my last entry, so listen carefully.

I'm looking at the wolfsbane.

Should I feed it to me>

Or should I feed it to him?

For the howling is close to my window now, a presence I cannot

shake.

I think he comes for me.

I know he comes for me.

And Dad can't help me now.